Frankenstein's Monster

*Also by J. S. Barnes
and available from Titan Books*

Dracula's Child
The City of Dr Moreau

Frankenstein's Monster

J. S. Barnes

after
MARY WOLLSTONECRAFT SHELLEY

TITAN BOOKS

Frankenstein's Monster
Print edition ISBN: 9781803362083
E-book edition ISBN: 9781803362953

Published by Titan Books
A division of Titan Publishing Group Ltd
144 Southwark Street, London SE1 0UP
www.titanbooks.com

First edition: September 2025
10 9 8 7 6 5 4 3 2 1

This is a work of fiction. All of the characters, organizations, and events portrayed in this novel are either products of the author's imagination or are used fictitiously. Any resemblance to actual persons, living or dead (except for satirical purposes), is entirely coincidental.

© J. S. Barnes 2025

J. S. Barnes asserts the moral right to be identified as the author of this work.

No part of this publication may be reproduced, stored in a retrieval system, or transmitted, in any form or by any means without the prior written permission of the publisher, nor be otherwise circulated in any form of binding or cover other than that in which it is published and without a similar condition being imposed on the subsequent purchaser.

A CIP catalogue record for this title is available from the British Library.

EU RP (for authorities only)
eucomply OÜ, Pärnu mnt. 139b-14, 11317 Tallinn, Estonia
hello@eucompliancepartner.com, +3375690241

Set in Bembo Std by Richard Mason.

Printed and bound by CPI (UK) Ltd, Croydon, CR0 4YY.

For Hugh

*"He was soon borne away by the waves,
and lost in darkness and distance."*

Frankenstein; or, The Modern Prometheus,
Mary Wollstonecraft Shelley

༺ ༻

On the thirteenth of April, 1852, my father – who was at that time a serving police officer in the City of New York – arrested, at the corner of Norfolk Street, not far from Tompkins Square, a vagrant in a state of bloodied distress. My father – who, I suppose, for the purposes of this narrative, I ought sometimes to call Charles (as that was his given name, though I could never think of him, then or now, as anything other than Pa) – approached the fellow with caution, but in a characteristic spirit of kindness.

For Sergeant Charles Wyatt always took a keen, empathetic interest in the underclass. He kept an eye on the comings and goings of derelicts and petty thieves, vagabonds, cut-throats and all the roving strangers who lived their lives in that great city on the cusp of lawlessness. He understood – and he taught me the same – that while acts born of desperation might not morally be considered as felonies in the same sense as plots of grand larceny, the world through which the poor and dispossessed had no choice but to move contained all that was needed to nourish lifelong criminality. On numerous occasions, he had intervened to help unfortunates and to raise them up out of their predicaments. He knew the one good, safe orphanage in New York and there are many children whom he rescued who owe their lives to his kindness. My father's most influential intervention saw him snatch away a young boy from the worst kind of life at the hands of guardians not worthy of the name. You would know of that rescued mite were I to name him here, for he is now said to be the most brilliant and promising congressman of his generation. This is what I choose to remember most often of my father's legacy – not the sad and broken figure he became.

All of which I lay before you so that you may understand that my father was no unworldly mark or gullible apprentice but also that he was not lacking in sympathetic understanding. The police force was then still in its infancy – a long way from what it is today – yet he knew the city and it knew him. When I recall him now (for he has been dead these past two years) it is almost as though he were an emanation of New York, a kind of mechanism of defence that had been created as the streets became ever larger and more populous, as the underworld just went on swarming.

Now, my father had seen the vagrant in question before. The man had appeared some months earlier, joining the huddled lines of his fellow tramps with a great and palpable unease, as though this were the very last place that he had ever expected to end up. He was a slim man with a drooping, pale moustache. His accent spoke of a fine American education and easy money which seemed impossible to fit together with the ruined figure he now cut. He had a marked distaste for physical contact of any kind and he positively shrank away from the touch of any other fellow, however kindly meant. My father had marked him out as one for whom the life of the streets would prove hard indeed and he had, among his many other duties, tried his best to keep a close eye on the new tramp's progress.

Yet good intentions do not always resolve themselves

into action. My father at that time was much occupied by a wave of killings which had startled and discomfited even the battle-hardened residents of the city, together with the usual cavalcade of petty criminality, with the result that he had lost sight of the new arrival more easily than he might have done in a quieter spell.

It was, then, with a small tug of guilt that my father approached the wild-eyed man that night, his hands outstretched before him in a gesture meant to soothe and calm.

The destitute was screaming. Crazy talk from the sounds of it, the ravings of a man whose sanity has worn too thin, though later my father claimed to be able to remember certain isolated phrases.

"The Mountain Gate... the Creature with the yellow eyes... the tap-tap-tapping in the outbuilding... like stone onto wood..."

None of this meant the slightest thing to my pa, of course – though, by the end of the night, all of these words would hold a far greater significance. He reacted, according to the dictates of his rudimentary training, by speaking calmly to the man and with something that sounded almost like affection.

"Tell me all about it," he said, moving closer. "Sit down and tell me everything."

At this, the derelict, who had been waving his arms and distressing the public for almost an hour, paused and at last drew a breath. His eyes were bleary and swimming with tears but he seemed to see something in my father – perhaps a kindred spirit? – and so lowered his voice to say words which, for all that they lacked then any discernible context, sent a shudder through my father as would a blast of winter air.

"He's followed me here."

With this, the fellow, now seemingly exhausted, all but fell to the ground. My pa stood over him and saw the extent of the man's injuries. His face and moustache were speckled and matted with blood. Cuts and grazes were in abundance. He looked as though he had been the recent victim of some sustained assault. Months of street-living were often sufficient to all but unseat the reason of the sufferer. An attack this vicious might well be enough to destroy it entirely.

"My friend?" said my father. "Who did this to you?"

The vagrant looked up, for all the world as though it were the policeman who was the real madman present. "I did. I thought it the best way… The only way… To get what I need…"

"And what do you mean by that? The only way?"

The man on the ground looked up and grinned. Three of his teeth were missing. "The only way to escape him," he said. "The only way to be free."

It was then that my pa noticed something on the sidewalk down by the lunatic's feet. It was a stout kind of scrapbook, bulging with papers.

The man noticed the object of my father's gaze and he grabbed greedily at the thing and hugged it close.

"What's that?" asked my pa. "Got to be important for you to have kept it with you all this time."

"Oh this?" There came another toothless grin. "This is everything. This is the story. And this is the truth. I put it all together. I stitched and I darned and I pulled tight the threads."

"Now that is interesting," said my father, still in that same easy tone. "Maybe you'll let me take a look?"

At this, the man eyed him with suspicion but also with a

measure of hope. "Perhaps," he said. Then, looking my father up and down: "Perhaps I will."

So my father arrested him and took him to the station-house, more as a kindness than anything else, for the night was chill and the streets were unfriendly. Even a few hours of respite would be enough to allow the fellow to calm himself more fully. My father could arrange food and drink, maybe even spare him a few cents.

The fellow came dutifully enough in the end. My pa always had a way with persuading the desperate.

At the entrance to the station, he asked the man his name, for the accuracy of their records.

The fellow gave him a queer, cunning look. "My real name?"

"If you'd be so kind."

"That's odd." He patted at his blood-flecked moustache. "For I haven't used it in a while. It's Jesse. Jesse Malone."

He did not wait for any reaction from my father but stepped forth into the station, from whence he was delivered into a cell which, if not exactly well-appointed, was at least dry, solitary and not uncomfortable.

Now the name of Mr Jesse Malone rang a distant bell in the memory of my father. He could not place it immediately, but it seemed to him to possess ominous associations all the same. Some scandal? Some hushing up? He could not readily recall. It was not, in fact, till he returned home again that night that the truth was served up to him, from no less distinguished a source than my mother.

He came in late, but Ma could never get fully asleep without him present in our apartment. Like most folk nowadays who marry officers of the law, she worried ceaselessly about him, and with good reason. I, who was only five years old at the time of these events, had no such qualms and slumbered peacefully in the room next door.

The arrival of my father brought my mother full awake and, as was their custom, she asked him about the progress of his day. He mentioned a few small incidents, keeping from her, as ever, the worst excesses of the job. At the end, he chanced to mention Malone who, so far as he knew, still lay resting in his cell some miles hence.

My mother who had, at my father's carefully filleted recitation of the day, began to slip into a contented drowse, now looked at her husband with a startled expression.

"So that's what became of him," she said.

"You know the name?" asked my father, who was not unaccustomed to discovering that his wife's New York knowledge outstripped his own in certain directions.

She raised an eyebrow. "I would've thought everyone did…"

"Didn't I tell you it rang a bell for me?"

My mother wrinkled her nose, a sure sign that she was teasing. "It should've done more than that."

"Come on, Molly, it's late!"

She shrugged. "He was a famous rich boy once, from a famous family who went half-mad with it. Several of his relatives were in asylums. Plenty of his ancestors in the ground who should've spent their lives in institutions too. But Jesse was different. He ran away from the whole thing and went to England. Made some strange friends there, by all accounts."

"I do remember, now that you mention it," my father said.

"But what's he doing sleeping like that in the city and making a nuisance of himself?"

"You'll have to ask him that," said my mother. "Though it can't be good. Anything that's brought him down so low as that... I expect he'll have quite a yarn to spin you."

"I expect he will," said my father, thinking of that weird scrapbook which the man had carried with him.

"Maybe you'll find out tomorrow," said my mother as she stretched and wriggled down into bed. And that was the end of their conversation.

The next morning there came upon the front door of our modest apartment a ferocious hammering sound, so loud and so insistent that it sounded almost violent. I recall being woken by it, and crying out in shock, and my mother coming into my room to comfort me. I remember hearing my pa's heavy tread to the door, the sound of it being opened and of their subsequent urgent conversation. I feel sure that he must have had a weapon with him, a knife or pistol behind his back. For few things are so unsettling to the American policeman than a wild knock on the door while the city is in uproar and it's barely light outside.

I remember hearing his voice, asking: "What do you mean by all this ruckus?"

Then came another male voice, one I recognised. "I'm sorry, Charles. But I thought you'd want to know."

My mother must have recognised the voice too for, at the sound of it, she released me from her embrace, rose and led me through to our little front room. There stood my father and a man who I knew as his closest friend from work – Louis Brand – a fine policeman and a patriot, who was shot dead ten years after this conversation, by a woman whose secrets he had discovered and had no choice but to expose.

On our threshold, Louis nodded. "Sorry to call so early, ma'am." He looked at me. He was a big man, I remember, clumsy and ungainly. "Son."

My mother looked at him directly. "It's to do with Jesse Malone, isn't it?"

The other policeman looked at my father, as if to ask just what exactly he had been telling his wife.

"I only mentioned it the once," my father said. "I swear."

Louis spoke to my mother. "You're quite right, ma'am, it is."

She tutted. "Soon as I heard that name again, I knew it would be trouble." She gave the assembled menfolk a look of something close to haughtiness. There were family stories (never proven) that we had once moved in more exalted circles, a few generations back and my mother sometimes had an air about her which spoke of the old country and of great houses. "There's something wrong with the Malones," she said. "Always has been."

My father looked at her oddly.

"You'd better come with me, Charles," said Louis. "It's going to get ugly if you don't."

Pa agreed that this was likely. He kissed my mother on the cheek and bent down to kiss me too, and that is the last thing that I can remember personally from that dreadful morning.

The rest my father told me years later, after the death of my mother, at a time when his own sanity had started to decline. He went with Louis, of course, back to the station, where Malone was still thought to be safely penned. He was greeted there, in the wide vestibule of the place, which was busy even at that early hour, by a slender, groomed kind of a man in an expensive suit and the sort of smile which seemed counterfeit.

"So you're the man who arrested him?" said this gentleman to my father.

"I am Sergeant Charles Wyatt, yes if that's what you mean."

"My name is Peter Coenraads," said the man. "I am fortunate enough to be the chief custodian of the Malone estate and fortune."

My father, who had taken an immediate dislike to the fellow, said: "Are you now?"

"For many years I have managed the estate on Mr Malone's behalf while he has been resident in Europe and pursuing his many philanthropic interests there. I was quite content to continue in my duties upon his sudden and unexpected return to America. Yet he vanished almost as soon as he came back. And I have been in search of him ever since."

"Is that right?" my father asked. "And just how hard exactly did you look?"

Mr Coenraads favoured him with the iciest of gazes. "Extremely hard. But when a man does not wish to be found…" He gestured around him. "Well, there are times when the most efficient course of action is simply to wait for him to… so to speak… wash up on shore."

Pa glared at him. "He's not well," he said. "His mind is unsettled."

Coenraads did not seem surprised by the news. "Then if you'll just take me to him, I will make sure he gets all the help he needs."

My father did not feel that he had much of a choice, for Louis had already assured him that Coenraads had presented his bona fides. He led the visitor to the cell, while Louis followed on behind.

There was plenty in my father's career which he could not set aside in his generally unhappy retirement, cases which nagged at him and victims whose memories he could not shake. Yet chief amongst them was what they found in that cell, the one to which he had brought poor Mr Malone the night before, thinking it to be a place of safety.

When he unlocked the door and stepped inside, with Coenraads and Louis Brand at his heels, it was to find the vagrant lying dead upon the floor. There were no obvious signs of violence or of self-murder. Yet there was such a look upon the man's face, one of absolute loathing and despair, that the sight of it lodged in my father's imagination where it never would be shaken free.

I asked my father, when I was an adult and he an old man, what he believed had caused the heart attack which killed Jesse Malone. Some vision, I had wondered, some hallucination from the man's disordered brain?

My father shook his head. He had another theory. "The bars of that cell looked out on the street, three stories up. Something climbed – yes, climbed – up the wall that night. It looked in and it whispered to him in the darkness and it scared Malone to death. God knows what it spoke to him after midnight, what hideous truths and lunatic revelations."

"But surely," I began, taking my time with the unfurling of logic, "such a thing is impossible? How could anyone ever climb so high? I've seen that wall and it's sheer. I guess... a bird might have landed there and looked inside. But never a living person."

At this my father looked at me with affectionate irritation, as though he thought me a fool, which indeed he did. "When exactly did I say 'living'?" he asked. "When did I say anything about that?"

Of course, at the time, there was a great deal of shock and lamentation at the discovery of Malone. Not from the two policemen, for they were well accustomed to sudden and unpredictable death, but from Mr Peter Coenraads who professed a sort of outraged grief at his employer's demise. The expression of relief which had flitted across his face, however, when he realised that his master was dead and gone did not go unnoticed by my father. It was for this reason, then, that he did not take in the least bit seriously the professional man's threats of imminent legal action for their failure to keep alive a prisoner in police care.

As they said their goodbyes and as the body of Malone was taken to the morgue, Mr Coenraads took my father aside and asked whether the rich man had left any effects behind him.

"He had almost nothing on his person," my father said. "So far as I could see, he was living in a state of complete penury. He was wearing rags, as you saw. He had just a few stones in his pockets which were taken from him at the desk."

"Was there anything else?" Coenraads said with an unkind, perceptive look on his face.

My father, who was, of course, thinking of the scrapbook again, decided, on impulse, to lie. "Nothing," he said.

Coenraads looked at him oddly, as though he suspected the truth, and for a moment my pa thought the man was actually going to call him a liar. Then Mr Coenraads nodded, no doubt already thinking of all that untouched money in a family trust which no longer had a single living, sane member of the family left to claim it. He thanked my father, even going so far as to shake hands with him and Louis and then he left the building.

There was a deal of clearing up to do and much else to occupy my father over the course of that long day. The details of it are lost to me now. At the end, he went to the desk, thinking to see the scrapbook for himself. It was waiting for him there, but so was Louis.

"Why didn't you tell our visitor about that book?" he asked, as my father reached for it and tucked it under his arm.

My pa told him a brief version of what he would later tell me. "Besides," he added. "I'm not sure it isn't evidence in a crime of some sort."

"Yes, but of what sort?"

To this my father did not have a ready answer. "Let me read this," he said. "And maybe I'll find out." His friend was looking at him, concerned.

"Trust me?" my father asked and, of course, Louis Brand agreed.

My father did not come home to us that night but went instead to an establishment he then frequented, a quiet Manhattan bar, which was to burn down in unhappy circumstances the following summer. Here he ordered his usual drink from a barmaid who knew him well (though not as well, my father promised me, as my mother had sometimes feared) and he took it into a corner along with that fat, queer book. He thought he would need liquor to face the thing in its entirety and in this at least he was right.

Sitting alone, he took a drink and looked at the strange object. It was a big, old volume, its stitching now ragged and coming loose. Inside was a jumble of text, some pasted in, some written directly onto the pages. There were many different hands – much seemed to be by Malone himself but there were clippings too, and letters and transcripts. The writing, which he took to be Malone's own, began as a firm, confident thing. By the end, the dead man's testimony had transformed into a rough diary and his writing had grown into a mad, spidery crawl, full of blotches and stains.

My father told me he often wished that he had taken the book to the stove that night, that he had just thrown it inside and watched it burn. He wished he had never so much as glanced at a single word of it. Yet books cannot be unread, can they? Or testimonies unseen. The learning of this lesson would cost my father dear indeed.

And so he took another swig of strong drink, turned to the very first page and, in the centre of the most advanced city on God's green earth, he began to read a tale of superstition and horror which he would, until then, have believed to have been impossible in this supposed modern and optimistic century.

Dr Frank Wyatt

NEW YORK,
OCTOBER 30TH, 1872

PART ONE

THREE SIGHTINGS*

---

* The title for this initial section of the scrapbook seems to have been added later by Jesse Malone. The handwriting is closer to the scrawl of the final diaries than it is to the more restrained and disciplined lettering of his Personal Testimony.

I

∽o∽

*Excerpt from a public lecture given
in Hamburg on March 5th 1838 by the
noted polar explorer, Bruno Rieger*[*]

I saw the tall man first in motion – a lean, dark figure moving fast across the ice.

I had risen early while the camp was still sleeping and I had walked a little way beyond it so that I might spend a moment in quiet contemplation and say a prayer for those great explorations which lay before us. I think, perhaps, that mine own eyes may even have been closed and that when I opened them again (my conference with the divine being done) I saw that weird stranger moving in the otherwise empty space before me, his solitary form stark against a bleak horizon.

His gait was swift, his outline sleek and determined. I knew

---

[*] You may think that Rieger is a questionable source given the scandals that dogged his later years, given his propensity for the bottle and the undignified nature of his death. Yet I believe this fragment of evidence to be sound. There is much more to come in these pages which will support his account. But, of course, you must make up your own mind.

from harsh experience how the snow in that place can be a false friend, how the glare of endless white can mesmerise a man into believing in things that have no true shape or substance. Yet it was then – and it is now – my sincere belief that I knew myself and the land well enough to comprehend the difference between mirage and fact.

Of course, I had heard the whispers and the many rumours. The peoples of that land, of whose culture and beliefs I had made sporadic study, had spoken of a beneficent stranger who moved amongst them, a being at ease upon the floes, a strange, indigent hermit who had made his home in the Arctic wastelands and who seemed to them to be hardier and more capable of survival even than the fiercest and most long-lived of those defiant, self-reliant peoples. As to how this being was supposed to live or the nature of his sustenance or shelter – all was unknown.

By then, I had begun to think this "Creature" some shared dream, made up of old stories and shadows and glimpses of wandering bears. Yet here he was, a being drawn, surely, from myth and folklore, thrust without question into the waking world. How fast he moved! And with what dexterity, given his awesome shape and size.

You know, my friends, that I am not a man who hesitates. Rather, I am by nature a man who strives. Yet something that morning gave me pause. I admit to you all without shame that I stayed where I stood far longer than I ought to have done, far longer than might all the long-dead heroes of my youth.

Behind me, in the distance, I heard the stirrings of the camp and the high-pitched whine of our dogs. I considered then turning back, telling my fellows what I had seen. And urging our general pursuit of the vision. Yet it felt very much to me as though I had no real choice in the matter but rather to hasten after the disappearing man, just as fast as I was able.

My dear friends, if there are any here present this afternoon who harbour the slightest ambition to explore the undiscovered reaches of our earth, I would solemnly urge you now not to emulate my example and ever do anything so foolish as to set off alone into the ice without companions, dogs or provisions, in chase of what might very well have proved to be some trick of the light or worse. Some roving ghost or hungry spirit.

To consign oneself to the mercy of the Arctic snow without so much as a glimmering of a plan is the very height of foolishness yet that was precisely what I did on the morning of June 18th last year, and it is due to the mercy of our God, and perhaps, to one other also, that I stand before you today to tell my tale.

The trek at first was simple enough, at least for one such as I, who possessed considerable experience in the navigation of such terrain. One of the oddest elements of travel so far north, especially to those who know the ceaseless chatter of our Western cities, is the absolute silence of the Arctic world when one is alone and the ice is still. It is glorious and terrible all at once.

The sky was clear that morning, no storms being promised, and I found that I almost enjoyed the experience of the hunt. Even on this pleasant afternoon today in the company of you all, I am still not certain if what I say is the truth or not, but it surely seemed to me in the early stages of that slow and snowy chase of ours that my quarry knew I walked behind him and even that he wished for me to catch him. He would at times reduce his pace and at others even pause altogether as though to assist me as I struggled to reach his side. I confess that I lost track of time and that, in my sudden single-mindedness, I failed also to understand the shifting and treacherous weather.

Two or three hours passed, perhaps, in this fashion, or more. I do not know the detail except to say that I became all at once aware of just two things: that the sky had darkened (always a sure promise of a tempest) and that the tall man had vanished. It was as though I were suddenly awakened from a dream and that I did so to discover I had walked in my slumber. I cursed aloud at my own foolishness, and I wondered bitterly what madness had taken me into its unforgiving grip.

I wheeled about, realising that I had lost now all sense of direction. It was as though I had been bewitched, lured abroad as were the mariners of antiquity drawn towards the rocks by sirens. Ahead of me was only snow and behind me the same. Then, from the sky, came a great swirling mass of whiteness pouring down. I stumbled and moaned in despair. New snow would cover my tracks and there was now no chance at all that my fellows would ever find me alive. I was lost and abandoned. Then I glimpsed something – a new form in the gathering blizzard. Yet it was not the tall man nor, alas, was it any of my party come in search of me.

It was a being of a different order entirely. A four-legged thing, a bear of white fur and fangs. It saw me, an enemy, in the heart of its territory, at the same instant as I set eyes upon it. Disorientated and afraid, I floundered and stumbled. The bear turned its snout towards me, showed its terrible teeth and loosed a cry of furious warning. The scent I remember too – the smell of warmth and blood and matted fur and death upon the icy breezes.

Ladies and gentlemen, in that moment I felt the absolute and unquestionable certainty that I was about to perish. Let me tell you now that there is no dignity in that understanding. My guts and bowels were in uproar, my eyes swam with tears and my imagination could present me only with a vision of my mother upon the last time that we had met, purse-lipped and disapproving, embittered by the hand which life had dealt her. I must have made some sudden motion for the bear acted as though it believed itself to be under threat. It roared again and then, without further warning, it sprang.

You may find what happened then to be most improbable. You may think me to be mistaken at best and a liar or a drunkard at worst. Yet I know precisely what it was that I saw. In the demi-second before the beast was upon me, some other shape sped past the periphery of my vision and hurled itself furiously against the creature.

Ladies and gentlemen, what a privilege it was for me, who stumbled back and watched open-mouthed from a handful of feet away, to witness the battle that ensued between the bear and my rescuer, the tall, dark man whom I had been pursuing.

Sometimes I see it still in my dreams. The white beast on its hind legs. The tall man grappling with it. Their titanic struggle. The sounds of their rage, of fist upon fur in this, their fearsome bout. At last, with a cry of triumph, the man hurled the bear to the ground. It whimpered once, then snarled but made no further move towards either of us. An instant later, it turned and loped away, defeated, into the white distance.

The tall man was out of breath. Panting, the sound did not strike me as altogether human. He was bleeding from cuts and lacerations, made by the claws of the snow bear. Closer then than ever before, I saw the true strangeness of him: his skin like sallow paper, his lips black, his eyes an unholy shade of yellow.

"Thank you," I said but my saviour merely shook his head.

"This is no land for men." His voice was peculiar indeed, a low, dark thing, full of depth and echo.

"But you…" I said. "What are you? How do you live? And for how long?"

The being smiled. "I have survived here for almost forty years. But my time in this place is ending now."

"Teach me," I said. "Show me how you live."

He shook his head. "Leave," he said, "and never return."

He said something else, some piece of advice or exhortation, but the storm intensified and his words were lost. Before I could ask him to speak again, I heard from afar voices, cries and shouts in English as well as in my mother tongue.

These voices, I recognised as belonging to my fellows. They were calling my own name. Without thinking, I called out also: "Over here! I am here, my friends! Here!" Then I saw them, their welcome forms emerging through the snow – half a dozen of the party come to discover me.

I turned to he who had rescued me from the storm and from the bear, but he was gone. All there was now was acre after acre of billowing white. His deep footprints, as I watched, were covered over at once.

There is no more to tell, ladies and gentlemen, than that. I know nothing further. I know not who that strange personage may have been nor how he came to reside in that place of isolation. I have never encountered him again but I can and I do say this: that whoever he was, he haunts my dreams still.

II

Letter from Captain Ezra Shale to
Captain Robert Walton, November 11th, 1838

Dear Captain Walton,

It has been a goodly number of years since last we spoke or even clapped eyes upon one another, and I dare say you never expected to hear from me again. In fact, I do believe it is quite possible that you do not recall me at all, so busy has been your distinguished life, sir, and so brief was that arduous portion of it in which we were daily acquaintances.

I am now a captain, sir, but in the year of 1799 I was a mere member of your crew on that vessel which set out, without success, to discover the northwest passage in the lands of ice. I was a awkward young fellow back then, ill at ease about my betters, and what I learned on that long voyage has stayed with me ever since. What a strange time it was for us all. What sights we saw! What miracles we beheld! What dreadful secrets did we decide to keep!

I hear that the years since have not been easy ones for you, sir. Still, I hope this letter of mine finds you in better health than is generally reported and that you have got for yourself now some measure of peace. If that is so, I almost hesitate to interrupt your happiness but we all made a promise, did we not, Captain? We all made a promise to tell one another if there were ever to be any fresh... sighting.

That is why I write to you now, Captain. I will be brief, sir, as I do not wish to place you under any undue strain. Suffice it to say, that I have risen to captain of my own vessel – the *Tennessee* – built for trade and commerce and, in her time, pressed into service as a whaling ship too. It gives me no pleasure, sir, to admit that my crew have been a quarrelsome and troublemaking lot, and poor navigators to boot. There were, under my command, several unsuccessful mutinies which marked us out as being amongst the worst upon the seas. It was in the wake of the last of these blundering insurrections that the incident which forms the basis of this letter derives. We had meant to be taking cargo to the port at Aberdeen but we had somehow contrived to drift considerably further north, beyond even the Shetlands and towards the Arctic Circle. By the time that we had recognised our error and the crew had been mollified yet again with money and with grog and with the promise of shore leave, we had lost whole days. There was no alternative but to correct our course and hope that we would not be too parlously late to our destination. The mood onboard was just as you can imagine: sullen and exhausted, in spite of everything.

This was how I came to be standing alone on deck on the evening of October 2nd of this year, when most of the crew was abed and lazing. I found that I needed peace and sanctuary. I had to lose myself in the sight of the sea and to hope for better times ahead. I stood alone, watching the waves. No land was before us and nothing lay in view. Then I saw a long, dark figure moving through the water.

My first fear was that it was a man overboard, for ill feelings persisted amongst the crew and violent scuffles were by no means uncommon. Yet this unexpected figure moved with purpose. It was no creature of the deep, but rather a man, one who seemed, impossibly, to be dogging our path through the very tip of Arctic waters and back towards the Scottish mainland.

He became aware of me then. He always did have some extra qualities of perception, beyond those of mortal men. He looked up and I swear that, even in the gloom and across that distance, I saw the flickering orbs of his burning yellow eyes. Then he was gone, diving deep, lost to darkness again. All I could hear was the roaring and the seething of that freezing ocean.

You know of whom I speak, sir. You know!

If you remember me at all then you will remember me as an honest and a steadfast man, and not one prone to fancy. I will not say more as to his identity, sir. Not here. For there are many who might intercept this letter and read it.

Though there is one more thing to add.

We made good time in the end and arrived safely into port. If the men grew skittish at shadows in the rest of our voyage or if they complained about rations going missing or other quirks and mysteries, I distracted them easily enough with talk of drink and women.

But then, early in the morning on the day we came into harbour I woke to see him standing at the foot of my bed, as terrible as ever he was in '99. What a grave and dreadful sight he made! Where had he been? How had he survived, that Creature? He spoke to me, his voice sonorous and grave, almost a human sound yet, in some fashion, not quite that.

"Captain," he said. "Thank you."

I blinked and rubbed at my eyes to assure myself I was not dreaming. "Why?" I asked in a state of confusion. "Why have you come back?" I flinched and looked away.

"Do you truly desire an answer?" he asked.

I told him that I did. He turned his baleful eyes upon me. "Bad dreams," he said, and then he was gone.

That voyage, sir, will be my last. For I grow old, and I have lost what was left of my taste for maritime life. One of my three brothers has an inn in Nottingham, and I do believe that I will join him in the running of it. The life there will be quiet but honest.

But I thought you should know, sir. I thought that I should write to you in memory of our promise made amid the ice so very long ago. Should we be worried? Ought we to be concerned that he lives and that he is returning? I do not know the answers.

God bless you, Captain, and keep you.

Ezra Shale

III

∾

Excerpt from A Contemporary Survey of
London Folklore *by Nathaniel Greene*[*]

It is often said that while London has birthed many strange stories, the strangest of them are born underground.

For the subterranea of the city is a place of darkness and secrets, a realm that was well known to our ancestors, lined, as it is, with the remnants of the Roman age and with the relics of the Anglo-Saxon dead. It is a world of crypts and of abandoned cellars, of silt and ancient coins. Of lost bronze and stone and old bones. It is the lair of rats and spiders and eels and worse. Spirits are often said to be seen by those who venture beneath the surface: the ghosts of lost children, of jilted maidens and of those who flung themselves into the river or else who were pushed there. Earlier centuries than ours are filled with

---

[*] There is something troubling in the coincidence of the identity of this author. You will see the irony in time. Suffice for now to say that I wonder whether Nathaniel Greene in some way called the disaster that was eventually to befall him by setting this story down, whether it was some dreadful, inadvertent act of invocation?

still wilder tales of encounters with boggarts and fairies and untrustworthy shades, beings that made impossible promises to the unwary down in the deep dank dark.

Yet, while conducting research for this present volume, I was most intrigued to discover that such accounts are not restricted to the distant past or to those who lived before our grandparents' grandparents. In the very year that I am writing[*], a most peculiar narrative was heard by this author from a reputable young working man named Reuben Carter.

Carter was a rough-hewn, red-headed fellow, who had worked upon the great Thames tunnel, that which was dreamed up by Marc Isambard Brunel (then continued by his most industrious son, and worked upon, in halting stages, since 1825). Encountered by your author while on an all too rare visit to the capital (country life being now my natural milieu), this man, Carter, tempted into talking to me by the generous application of ale, told of how he and a friend (now sadly deceased) were working one night on the very last of the tunnel.

Others elsewhere can tell of those many men who died in the construction of this sunken folly, of all that blood and treasure which was given over in order to connect one bank of the river to another, as once the Babylonians sought to connect the Euphrates. Both of the workers in my story – Carter and his friend, whose name I never learned – had already lost others to accidents, to gas explosions, to fire and to dysentery. Carter's friend had lost an eye. He himself, he said, still woke in the night, crying "Flames! flames in the depths!" Yet they both worked on, for they had few other opportunities and little choice.

---

[*] I believe this to have been around the autumn of 1842.

On the night in question they were alone in that stretch of tunnel which lay directly beneath Wapping. It was late and the light from their guttering lamps was poor. No doubt both men were tired almost to the point of exhaustion, and no doubt there are many who will say that they were simply mistaken in what they claim to have seen, that their vision was the product of fatigue and gin-sodden imaginations. Yet such cynics have done not as I have done and looked into a man's eyes and heard Reuben Carter speak of the horror in the tunnel, of that inhuman thing that he glimpsed there.

The incident itself was brief and arbitrary, as is so often the way with the inexplicable. An irregularity was glimpsed by Carter in the flickering gloom by the earthen wall of the tunnel. A pause. A frown. A closer look. And then… the outline of what looked like a human figure… Carter, crying out to his friend: "Come! See here! What is this thing?"

Then the hurrying over and the holding up of the lamp. The gasps and coarse expressions of surprise. As to what it was that they saw there, the last living witness' own words will linger long in my imagination:

"It were a man, sir," said Carter to me above the sounds of revelry in the inn where we had met. "A man caught there, as though he had died long ago and been trapped in the clay ever since. Or else… like he was some old statue or sculpture. We have been known to find such things. But something about it, sir, put me in mind of a great fly drowsing in a spider's web."

I asked Mr Carter to describe this figure in greater detail.

"He was a man in aspect, to be sure, sir, but he was not… like us. He was very tall and very lean. His hair was long and lank and black. His eyes, sir, though half-closed were of a yellow sort. He seemed an impossible thing to us yet somehow he was possessed of *substance*... yes, sir, of *substance* that could not be denied. He was no ghost or elf or sprite, but a real thing which once had walked about the earth."

As Carter explained it to me, he and his associate then proceeded to gaze in awe and wonder for several long minutes upon this incredible sight. There seemed to be no ready explanation, no obvious means by which the stranger could have come there. Nor, I think, according to their testimony, was there any scientific method by which the body might have been so meticulously preserved. And so they stood there, those two Englishmen, and they watched and theorised, both afraid, yet both unwilling to turn their backs upon this hideous discovery. Carter told me that, thinking of his boyhood, he murmured a prayer of protection beneath his breath.

At length, it was decided that they should both go for help, find some of their fellows and report on what they had seen. Yet no sooner had they made this arrangement and moved, with great and understandable hesitancy, away, than they heard a sound which, Carter told me, he would never forget for as long as he lived.

It was the sound of movement behind them, of something detaching itself in dreadful increments from the wall. It was a sound of sucking yet also of unearthing, like some gigantic insect might make, some winged titan burrowing through the earth.

At this noise, the two men clasped at one another, like children alone in a forest. Then, with courage which astonishes me at the mere thought of it, they turned around to see what they already suspected to be the truth: that the figure of the tall, dark man now stood upright in that dim tunnel and was moving towards them with a speed that was as surprising as it was impossible. Neither man dared to block its path. The weird being swayed past them and out into the tunnel beyond, making as it did so a growl of what sounded like outrage. Carter told me that, as the being processed beside him, he caught the scent of loam and sea-salt and decay. It all happened swiftly, I was told, horribly swiftly and in a swirl of dense shadow.

I recount this tale here chiefly as a means of demonstrating the persistence of certain folk beliefs in the metropolis and as a fragment of possible interest to the antiquarian, making no claim whatever for its accuracy. Needless to say, I was able to find no other worker to corroborate the story of Reuben Carter and his friend.

Carter himself cannot now be traced. Upon my most recent visit to the metropolis, he could not be found. His neighbours in Rotherhithe informed me only that they had not seen him for some weeks and that he had, of late, taken to telling them how tired he had become of the city, of how he longed now for peace, as far away as possible from London and from her great and terrible river.

PART TWO

THE PERSONAL TESTIMONY OF JESSE MALONE*

---

* I believe this to have been written in a short space of time in the autumn of 1850. There are signs of that hereditary madness which would fell poor Malone in the end, but they are at this stage mere disquieting oddities.

I

As I write, I find myself gravely concerned about the fate of my friend, the Englishman, Mr Hubert Crowe.

In the course of our acquaintanceship, I often thought him mad and sometimes a charlatan. What terrifies me now is the thought that he may indeed have been right all along and that, in consequence, his soul is in the worst kind of danger. I fear also that he has walked into a bear-trap, one designed with cunning for him and him alone, one which will show him no mercy and leave any who care for him entirely bereft.

But I ought to begin properly, I should lay things down in as orderly a way as I can manage. I should be plain, and I should tell you everything.

II

My own name is Jesse Malone. I am forty-two years old now and originally a native of New York City, though I have crossed the Atlantic but once, when I was three and twenty. Ever since, I have made my home in the venerable settlement of London, taking up a set of rooms in a crumbling tenement in the district of Clerkenwell.

I lost my parents at a young age: my mother to a peculiarly urban strain of fever when I was barely old enough to walk and my father to a hereditary insanity which saw him removed to an asylum when I was seventeen.

Such details are barely relevant to this account but let it suffice here to say that it was in part a desire to escape from the family taint which claimed my father that led me to flee our United States of America to seek solace and security in the old country. In this, I believe that I have been successful for I have noted in myself so far no signs of that which bedevilled so many of my ancestors.

England has kept me sane. Something about its great antiquity and the perspective on one's own existence that is granted by its constant reminder of age has allowed me for years now to live a life of quiet, rational sobriety.

At least, this had been the case until last year when I first encountered Mr Hubert Crowe.

III

If that persistent frailty in our mental faculties is the worst element of my inheritance, perhaps the best, or at least the most useful, is a private income which is permitted by that minor fortune which was amassed by my forebears in colonial days. It has allowed me to live as I wish to live and it has provided a welcome shield from the world.

My existence has always been a modest one, meaning that the money has lasted very much longer than it might have done in the hands of some more spendthrift fellow. I have spent a good deal of it not upon myself but in the pursuit of fairness and happiness in the lives of others, in discreet works of philanthropy.

Since 1835, I have contributed much to the poor of the

city. I have wandered a great deal into the lowest alleys and the vilest rookeries (for such is the term here for their close-packed, almost inhumane settlements) and I have seen plentiful sights to chill the imagination and quicken the beating of the heart.

I have given away in small slices a goodly proportion of my personal wealth, both as one individual to another and, in recent years and with increasing frequency, as part of a greater organisation. You may have heard of it: The North American Assembly for the Improvement of the London Poor.

I am a founder member – one of six such gentlemen, all born in the land of the free and now resident here in the motherland – and I do believe that we have done much to alleviate the sufferings of so many unfortunate souls who have been lost to the reaches of the city.

In this capacity I have become, I dare say, as great an expert in the workings of London life as any who is not a native can be.

My position at the Assembly has also granted me access to a great number of institutions which do what they can to stem the rising tides of poverty and want: the prisons, the ragged schools and the workhouses. The Assembly is well known to the law and we are sometimes called upon to act as a "go-between" for the authorities and the everyday people, most of whom are suspicious and afraid of any who might wield power over them. It was as a direct result of my position at the Assembly, that I first met the man whose name hangs, heavy as a shroud, over this account.

IV

The date is graven on my memory: 2nd February, 1849.

I had slept poorly – unusual for me then, though now a commonplace thing – and I had risen later in the day than was good for me. I had that unpleasant sense of my time being half-wasted when, having eventually risen and washed, I saw through my window that we had no more than a few hours left of daylight.

The woman who takes care of my set of rooms and who keeps a good house for me (Mrs Armitage is her name) knows better than to disturb me so I knew the matter must be serious when, just after three o'clock, she knocked on my door and called out, her voice full of what to an American ear (however far from the motherland) still sounds full of misplaced consonants – "Mr Malone! Mr Malone, sir! Are you there? Are you well?"

I went at once to the door and flung it open to find the woman shivering on the threshold, her eyes speaking of recent tears, fretful and afraid. She was in general a stony one so I was much surprised to find her in so reduced a state.

"Mrs Armitage, whatever is the matter?"

I have been told that I have a calm manner as might befit a sawbones or a preacher, though on that long afternoon this did nothing at all to soothe her.

I am not a gentleman known to offer or to enjoy the touch of any other, preferring to keep myself separate and apart, yet I saw in that instant no alternative but to lean forwards, place my left hand on this lady's shoulder, squeeze once and murmur: "There, Mrs Armitage. You surely have to tell me what the matter is."

Her words came out in a rush. "Course, sir, the worst

thing about it is that I *knew* him, sir… I knew him! I can just remember him… running happily… he had such a lovely laugh, sir… and two clear blue eyes just as pretty as a picture…"

I asked the woman who she was talking about and why these memories (as they seemed to be) had plunged her into such distress. Yet she barely seemed able to hear me and simply went on.

"So difficult a life, sir… that little lad… his bonny little legs… and his smile, sir… such a smile as would lift up the hearts of angels."

"Mrs Armitage!" I could see no alternative course of action but to raise my voice to an uncharacteristic degree. "Come now. Calm yourself. And tell me – whatever has happened?"

She stopped, bit her lower lip and looked at me, chastened and almost shocked at my unexpected timbre.

"Please," I said, more gently this time. "Tell me."

V

The tale came out of her then in a great, unseemly rush, full of hesitations, euphemisms and garbled misunderstanding. I do not propose here to even attempt to write it down as it was spoken to me but instead to summarise it so that you can comprehend the nature of the thing.

A young boy had gone missing: a child by the name of Simon Olney.

His mother – a poor woman who dwelled in one of the most impoverished parts of the city – was known to us both, to me by way of my charitable endeavours, and to Mrs Armitage through some complicated lattice of cousins and relations by marriage which I could never seem to grasp in its entirety.

He was barely five years old, this Simon Olney, but more intelligent and lively than one had any right to expect given his rude start in life. I am not a gentleman who would ever seek or enjoy the company of the young but Olney was an exception, a singular child, unusually bright and perceptive. According to my housekeeper, he had not been seen then for two days and two nights, lost somewhere in the wilderness of London and his poor mother was beside herself with fear and worry.

Was there anything I could do to help that poor family, she wailed, was there anything at all?

In truth, I doubted that there was much which lay within my power, being neither a native nor the kind of man who possesses the necessary gifts of investigation. Yet there was something, something about that boy and his family which drove me to pledge to Mrs Armitage that I would go at once to the home of the Olneys and put myself entirely at their service in the search for their child.

In such moments of decision are whole chains of incident set in motion, in such sudden judgements are planted the seeds of tragedy.

VI

The next hour passed in a haze of activity and frustration.

I threw on a coat and boots and went out at speed into the thin grey rain of that February afternoon, for once barely conscious of the elements, with Mrs Armitage's entreaties still, as they say, "ringing in my ears".

Despite the rain, I found a cab that would take me as far as Spitalfields. From there I walked, as the rain worsened, to a street at the tip of Whitechapel where the Olneys resided in a state of poverty but a rung or two removed from utter indigence. The name of the street was Allan's Row and it was as mean a line of fever-haunted tenements as ever I saw in the worst stews of New York.

They lived halfway along this morose avenue and, as I passed the many heaps of rags which stirred when I went by, I felt the gaze upon me of sundry surly eyes, staring out from behind shattered glass. At the house of the Olneys there was no reply, nor any sign of life. I was, for a moment, quite lost until I heard the grind of an ancient windowpane, and a voice call out to me that if it were the Olneys I was wanting they were in the church to pray for the recovery of their boy. There was a slam above me before I could thank the unseen speaker.

Back along the street I went, and back towards the church at Spitalfields about which there always hangs a pall of misery, a high, cold structure, more like a beacon than a temple. Here, once again, I could see no sign of the Olneys, though there were any number of beggars who lay in wretched supplication at the feet of the steps. A prelate emerged at my insistence, his face swollen and bruised as the result of some recent fracas and he told me, through thick and bloodied lips, that the family of the Olney boy had indeed been there and that they had received some news of his whereabouts. He told me where they had said they were headed and so I thanked him and walked on again. I found another cab and set off across London, following Great Eastern Street to the Euston Road, moving through Shoreditch, Angel and Euston itself, in the teeth of a grim, relentless downpour, arriving eventually (and, I see now, inevitably) at the gates of The Regent's Park.

There was some disturbance at the main gate. A knot of ragged people seemed to be endeavouring to gain entrance while those who guarded it – four burly fellows in uniform – pushed them back to keep them out and seemed on the very edge of moving to further violence. Recognising some of those who were being denied entrance, I paid the driver and stepped back out into the rain to help.

I saw immediately the nature of the dispute. Mrs Olney was at the head of the group, a half dozen family members in her wake. The chief warden, a fat man with a shock of grey hair was barring her way; the whole affair was becoming ugly.

I began to intervene, assuring the park men of my credentials and offering to reach for my pocketbook while trying also to secure from the missing boy's mother or from any of her familiars, exactly what she was doing here, so far from home, and what precisely had led her to this place at this darkening hour, begging to be let inside. I could get no clear answer to any of it, for all were speaking at once, and, as the rain poured now, pure chaos seemed inevitable. Then, from out of the storm came a low, determined voice.

"Mrs Olney! I know the location of your son!"

Something in the quality of that voice made us all stop and turn to see this new arrival.

A figure stood before us in the driving rain, an unexpected silhouette in the twilight.

And that was the first time I ever laid eyes on Mr Hubert Crowe.

VII

He did not look like a madman. My suspicions on that score came later. In fact, he did not look in the least bit out of the ordinary. He was small and plump, about my own age. His face was unshaven and exhibited such rare irregularities of feature that an unkind observer might describe him as being on the very edge of misshapen. Certainly, in his worst moments he had something about him of the stout old English gargoyle, stepped down from some cathedral, who'd taken to wandering the streets. His eyes danced brightly, and his voice spoke of education. Yet there was no time that night for any but the most cursory observation of the man for no sooner had he spoken than poor Mrs Olney, by now half-crazed with grief and fear, ran to him, sobbing: "Who are you, sir? Where's my boy? Where's my little boy?"

As she reached his side, the newcomer pointed towards the gates. There was no need for any further explanation. The gaze of the stranger passed over Mrs Olney and the assembled rabble before alighting on me. I dare say it is a trick of my memory, but it seemed that they stopped there with something of a jolt, as though he recognised me, as if I were already known to him.

He looked me firmly in the eye and shouted above the sound of the rainfall.

"You! Come with me, please!"

He did not wait for my response but strode on towards the gates of the park. I followed, somehow without question, caught up already, though I did not yet know it, in the peculiar gravity of Hubert Crowe.

VIII

I find that I cannot write easily or lightly of what came next. It has for me now certain aspects of a dream or nightmare. I remember following Crowe to the gates. I remember him riding roughshod over the protestations of the guards and pushing his way beyond them. I remember the sight of that ungainly fellow breaking into something almost like a run or, at least, a kind of urgent, clumsy scuttle. I remember following him further into darkness and rain. I remember the lack of light, the earth sodden and slippery beneath our feet. I remember the man who was first ahead of me and then by my side (as even I am fleeter of foot than he) calling out the name of the Olney boy.

"Simon! Simon!"

His voice sounded dull and flat against the mass of trees and the downpour. I remember feeling despair wash over me at the realisation that I was doing nothing more than blunder in the dark in search of a boy who might be anywhere in London or beyond — who might, if I were to be wholly honest with myself, no longer be counted amongst the living.

Yet Mr Crowe seemed possessed of some inner compass.

On he went in his clumsy but determined fashion.

"Where are we headed?" I shouted, more than once.

"The boy!" is all he called back. "The Olney boy is close!"

I could prise no more sense from him than that yet still we ran on. Once I slipped and he helped me to my feet. Once he did the same and I wrenched him to his. A few startled animals crossed our path, once a deer, once a wild dog of some description which snarled at us before loping away.

The rain grew worse and the night drew tight around us.

When I fell for a second time, it was into a patch of mud and brambles.

I cursed and swore as I staggered up, and as the man reached out his hand to me.

"Enough!" I said. "This is a damn foolish waste of time. The boy could be anywhere."

As I regained my balance and drew in a panting breath, he cried out: "The boy is nearby, Mr Malone!"

"How can you possibly know that," I began, then added: "and how do you know my name?"

Crowe wiped his forehead with his plump right hand, making little difference to the great quantity of rainwater which had accumulated there.

"I can answer your first question," he said, "though as to the second... I find I am... unsure..."

He sounded perplexed, which I have considered many times since to be a thing most odd. "I'm Crowe," he said. "Hubert Crowe."

"Malone," I replied. "But then you know that. Besides, we should leave. This search is fruitless. This whole affair is—"

And that is when we heard it. High above the sounds of the storm, the thin, pitiful cry of a little boy, crying out for help. We turned and ran towards the origin of the noise and we found him — at last — at the foot of an oak tree, wet through, shivering and incoherent. I have no doubt at all that a night alone in that place would have killed him as surely as would a noose.

"Come here." Mr Crowe stretched out his hand.

The boy stared up out of the dark. His clothes were as rags, I saw, and his face grimy. There was a cut above his right temple.

"Simon?" I said. "Come here."

He came to us then, reluctant, fearful and babbling, and fell almost at once into a swoon.

And so it was that Mr Crowe and I came to walk together through the gates of the park, carrying that poor little boy between us.

I will leave you to imagine the response that we received from his mother and his family, the cries and cheers and many questions and thank yous.

Much of it is faded now in my memory, clouded by all that came after.

But it was a happy moment all the same and it occasioned the first smile that was exchanged between me and Mr Hubert Crowe, he whose life and sanity hangs now, I do believe it, by the very slimmest of threads.

IX

"So how the Devil did you do it?" I asked, somewhat regretting the use of the word "devil". "How did you know where the boy would be?"

The two of us had found a cab, loitering a short distance from the park gates. The hour was late by then, once we had said our farewells to the assemblage and seen that bewildered little boy borne lovingly away. Yes, the hour was late and the storm had barely relented so it was natural enough, after our long ordeal, that Mr Crowe and I should have sought sanctuary and transport together.

We shouted out to the driver almost as one and clambered

with gratitude on board. The fellow seemed dazed and unsure of himself and, though I wondered at first if he were drunk, he soon rallied and appeared happy enough for the fare.

And so we found ourselves together, Mr Crowe and I, side by side, being driven through the London streets.

Crowe smiled at my question, though the smile was of an exhausted kind. "I could tell you easily enough," he said, "though I somehow doubt that you'd believe me."

"You might be surprised," I said. "For I believe myself to be a worldlier fellow than I appear."

Crowe looked at me closely. "Too late tonight," he said, "to explain. Besides, you would most likely think me a madman."

"Oh?" is all that I said in reply to that, and "is that so?"

I was thinking, of course, of certain of the wilder branches of my own family tree.

For a few long minutes there was just the swaying of the carriage, the sound of hoofbeats, the surly city rushing by.

"If you wish to understand, you can call tomorrow. In the afternoon. As late as you are able."

He did not wait for my reply but only closed his eyes, after that slunk down into his seat and laid his feet further out before him. I did the same for sleep now threatened to overwhelm me.

At Clerkenwell, as I was about to step out, he stirred. One eye twitched open. A plump hand was flung outwards, in its palm a small card. He did not speak. I pocketed the item and clambered back out towards home.

It was not until much later – once I had bathed and reassured Mrs Armitage, and felt at least a little more human – that I inspected the card in earnest. His name was written there, of course, as was an address: 111 Pilate Court, Southwark. But then below this was a single word which I found both curious and obscurely troubling.

"Prophet."

X

I have ever been a solitary gentleman, a person who does not seek the company of either sex, and one who often shrinks from social intercourse of any kind. Yet somehow there was no doubt at all in my mind that I would accept that invitation.

On the morning after the return of Simon Olney to his mother, I rose late, aching and still exhausted. I had work to do for the Assembly and a conversation to have with Mrs Armitage, one of uncomfortable duration in which she rehearsed again her gratitude at the safe homecoming of the child and shared such news as she had received from that family as to his recovering spirits and general resilience.

It was with some relief that I left my desk at shortly after three, dined, swiftly, and took myself to Southwark in order to present myself at number 111 Pilate Court and to meet again its puzzling inhabitant.

I found the place to be a low, mean dwelling, situated in a courtyard adjacent to a row of grim, unpatronised shops: a fruiterer, a pawnbrokers and an establishment which seemed to stock nothing other than line after line of glass bottles. The house lay in its furthest corner and had evidently been divided, by some more than usually greedy landlord, into three separate apartments – numbers 113, 112 and 111.

All of them shared a common entrance and a single bell, an arrangement which must have caused a great deal of confusion and inconvenience. I should perhaps have felt surprise at finding my new acquaintance in so restricted a set of surroundings but somehow I was not. For I had, from the first, seen in him an edge of something less than well-mannered, a familiarity with what lies half-hidden in the city, an understanding of the mud beneath the water.

I knocked at the peeling green door and waited. At once, heavy footsteps sounded, moving swiftly towards me. I stepped back. The door opened and I was confronted not by Mr Crowe but by a woman, advanced in years and dressed in several coats and woollen garments as if intending to go out into a heavy snowstorm. Her feet were clad in slippers and I found myself unsure as to how she could possibly have been the authoress of that determined stamping which I had heard but a minute before.

Her face was wrinkled. She wore a pensive look.

"Jebediah?" she asked and, to my surprise, I realised that her accent spoke of the Southern states of my own nation. "Is that you?"

"I'm afraid not, ma'am," I said. "My name is Malone."

She squinted at me. "You a friend of Jebediah's then?"

I raised my hands in a gesture of regret. "I do not know that gentleman, ma'am. I am here to visit with a person named Hubert Crowe."

"Hmm." She looked at me doubtfully then turned her back and called into the shadowy depths of the house. "Elijah! Oh… Elijah!" Her voice, when raised, had a high, crooning quality. I wondered at her sanity. "There's a man here to see you." She gave me a look of real craftiness and said: "I call your friend Elijah, you see... on account of those visions of his. That and the fiery chariot which swept him up to heaven."

More footsteps came then and Crowe himself emerged from some steep, subterranean flight of stairs, red-faced and out of breath. "You came," he said, without emotion.

"Here I am."

"Your assistance last night," he said, "was invaluable."

"Not at all. I was very happy to help."

He nodded at me and I nodded back, and an awkward silence reigned, at least until the old woman interrupted.

"You know this one, Elijah?"

"Yes, yes, I do, thank you, Miss Nash. Always comforting to know that you guard the gateway."

She shot him a look of irritated suspicion. "I don't believe I care for him," she said, with an odd flatness of tone, "I don't think he will prove to be good for you." With this, she shuffled away.

I looked at Crowe and raised an eyebrow.

"This way," he said. "Follow me. After all, you said you wanted an explanation."

"I did."

"Well then, you've arrived at an interesting moment. I am in the midst of a divination. Come this way and I'll introduce you to the cards."

These last two words seemed at the time strange but innocuous, yet they were to change the course of my own life, first for the better and then, with a series of horrible lurches, for the worse.

XI

In recent days, I have often wondered how different things might have been had I turned then on my heels, made some vague excuse and walked away from that unhappy structure, with its madwoman at the door and its atmosphere of decay and contradiction. Would I have been content to learn nothing more of my new acquaintance and simply return to my old life?

Perhaps I would not – perhaps there would have remained a certain restlessness in my character – but surely that would have been better than the path down which my association with Hubert Crowe was to lead us?

"Come on," said Mr Crowe and, placing his hand upon the small of my back, steered me gently along a hallway that had been painted a faded shade of red towards a flight of stairs which led to blackness, where a gentle flicker was the only promise of illumination. "Down here," he said. "Visitors first."

"Is it your office?" I asked.

"And my home."

I walked down the stairs, each of them creaking in protest. I heard Crowe move behind me.

At the bottom of the stairs was a darkened vestibule and beyond this was a large, plain chamber which looked something like a drawing room. There was a mirror on one wall and an ugly seascape on another. The air smelt of sweet scented smoke.

Two other closed doors led away from it. In the centre of the room was a table, with a seat on either side. A sheet of black satin lay upon the table, and on that sheet of satin were what seemed to me to be five large playing cards, all of them placed face down.

"Here." Crowe gestured to the chair that was the closest to the exit. "Please take a seat."

I sat, feeling like a child brought up onto stage.

"Look down!" prompted Mr Crowe, as he took the chair that was opposite to me.

I looked and saw before me five large rectangles of thick card stippled with light blue dots.

"These are playing cards?" I asked, though they seemed far bigger than any that I had seen before. That sense, of being part of a stage act, came back.

"No, not quite. They are of my own design. I was about to see what they might wish to tell me today."

"I'm not sure that I understand your meaning."

"You saw my calling card," Crowe said simply. His gaze was cool and level. "You saw what it said."

As I replied, I could feel myself moving further into the unknown, like a nervous bather, up to his ankles in some lagoon, now stepping anxiously into deeper water. "It said… prophet."

"A slightly colourful description. But I find it captures the imagination of my clients."

I must have looked askance at the appearance of this final word for he spread wider his hands in a gesture of half-mocking apology. "I was born into something, Mr Malone, not so very far removed from poverty. My circumstances, as you can see, are even now of a restricted sort. I have need of those who will pay for my services."

I felt, not for the first time, a moderate flush of unjust shame for all the wealth that had been bequeathed to me.

"What is it you…" On the cusp of saying "claim to be able

to do?" I stopped my speech in time and finished it instead with: "are you able to provide?"

There was complete gravity in his eyes and no obvious lie there that I could perceive. "I can see the future. Glimpses and shards, at least. Enough to understand patterns in particular events, to see... the shapes of them."

"Divination achieved by reading the cards?" I said, with an odd, forced lightness of tone. "You find that more reliable than, say, watching the flight of birds? Or of sifting through entrails?"

It was the one and only time I ever dared to apply levity to the talents of Mr Crowe. He looked at me with an air of disappointment, which put me in mind of an old college tutor of mine.

"Scepticism is forgivable. Yet I have had some successes."

"May I ask what those were?"

"Objects located. Deaths and marriages predicted." He blinked, a thing he did, I was to learn, when pushing aside some strong emotion. "True feelings for another revealed for what they were. Besides, before you came today I asked to see what the future would hold for you and I."

"For us?" I said, with some surprise.

"I asked whether this would be our only meeting or if we are meant in some fashion, following our recent success, to join forces."

"Oh?" I said. "And what did they show you?"

"I have yet to see for myself. Let us look together. Touch the bottom card, Mr Malone, if you would be so kind, with the fingertips of your left hand."

Wondering if I hadn't been somewhat disrespectful, I did

what he said. The card was smooth and still warm. Was there a quality to it even of something like vibration? No, I thought surely there could not be. And yet…

"Turn it over."

Of course, I performed this action.

"The first card," said Mr Crowe, "shows what has been."

I looked down and saw there an ornate, quaint painting of a robed man on horseback. It was an original piece of work, clear and vivid but with something indefinably troubling about it.

"The Pilgrim turns to War," said Crowe.

"I beg your pardon?"

"It is the name of the card," he said.

"Oh? Is it now? And what does that signify?"

"It has… various meanings. But I do believe in this instance that it shows us an element of you."

"Of me?"

"Next card, please."

An unexpected solemnity lay between us now. I turned over the second card.

"This," said Crowe, "is how things are."

I looked at the image – painted as gorgeously as before but this time a little darker in hue, and with a greater concentration of shadows. It showed a doorway in a crumbling wall, opening onto a half-glimpsed landscape of fantastic peaks and mist-shrouded valleys.

"The Mountain Gate," Crowe said. "New beginnings. New alliances. A new journey to take."

"And what does the third card show?" I asked, though I had already guessed something of his answer.

Crowe was like a priest giving communion. "The future," he said. "The most dangerous of the three."

When I turned over the final card, I admit I gasped at the image that was shown there. Nothing in the first two portraits could have prepared me for the absolute grotesquerie of this last image, for its abiding quality of determined malevolence. Crowe himself said nothing and I saw that he was gazing down at it with fear.

"Ah," he said eventually. "That has never been drawn before. I painted it, in a half-fever once, under the influence of… well, let us just say that it is not a thing I care to look at closely."

I glanced again at the third card, and I still could not suppress a shudder. It showed a creature of the most hideous kind – something like a frog of impossible dimensions, the size of a horse but with eyes that peered with dreadful hunger out of a pitted face with a horribly human aspect. It squatted in gloom and filth in some underground place and there was something at its side – some half-finished meal – a description of which I dare not commit to paper.

"I can't say I am surprised," I said. "Wherever did such an image spring from? From what dark depth of your imagination?"

Crowe shook his head. "It is not a question of imagination. They are not my own notions. Rather I am a conduit for a deeper, more distant well."

"Disgusting," I said, though I could not wrench away my gaze. "It's… that thing… it's disgusting…"

"It has a name," said Crowe. "It is the demon Antenar. That was what the Hebrews called him. The Assyrians, the Canaanites, the Ancient Egyptians all had others. It has been with us for long centuries now, a thing of blood and shadow. It portends no good. It loves nothing more than to forge a chain of disparate yet related events and watch as they move towards tragedy."

I looked away and did my best to smile at my host. "Mr Crowe," I said, rising to my feet, "it has been a great pleasure to meet with you. What you did yesterday was remarkable. And I would like to thank you for that from the bottom of my heart. But I have a great many responsibilities and it is to them which I must now return." I did not extend my hand but only nodded and turned to leave.

Crowe blocked my path to the door.

"I suppose you must think me insane?" he asked colourlessly and without the least hint of rancour.

That thought, of course, was most certainly in my mind by then – even after what I had witnessed the night before. "No," I said. "Not at all."

"I do understand how it must seem to you, Mr Malone. Like a parlour trick, like a piece of whimsy or the work of a mountebank."

He stopped himself and took a breath. "The cards led me to that boy. You know that. They pointed me towards the park and to that very region of it."

"I have no doubt you saved that boy's life," I said. "I thank you for it. As do we all."

"Yet you doubt the efficacy of the cards?"

"How... how on earth could they have shown you?"

The man seemed truly perplexed by my question. "The cards were quite clear," he said. "The Steeple was first. Then the Heart of the City. Then the Woodsman."

Having come reluctantly to the conclusion that the fellow was every bit the lunatic that he professed not to be, I smiled, nodded and moved gently a pace or two towards the door. "As I say, it's really been most interesting to meet you, Mr Crowe."

He looked a little saddened but he stepped aside for me. "And you too, Mr Malone."

As I reached the door I heard him sit again at the table. I heard the rippling sound of his shuffling the cards.

"Good luck to you, sir," I called back, my fingers on the door handle. In swift succession I heard the sound of three cards being dealt. Then I hesitated, for something within me did not wish to leave that room.

A moment of stillness passed then Crowe said, very softly and with great kindness: "You were not born alone, were you?"

A shiver went through me. "What did you say now?"

"You were a twin. There was another – a little boy. Taken into heaven when he was still so small."

For a long moment, no sound was made. Crowe spoke the truth though to have done so was quite impossible. I had told no-one in more than thirty years about my brother. There was not a man left alive who could have known.

"The cards," Crowe said. "They tell me that he is with you, even now, at your side."

"He is," I said and my voice sounded very dull and faraway to me. "In spirit and in memory."

I heard Crowe stand up and pace towards me. I had the sudden presentiment that he meant to touch me, some manly squeeze of my shoulder or sympathetic hand. I turned to face him.

He stood before me, smiling sadly. "Sometimes it is more than that, is it not? More than a memory. And more than an echo."

I took a pace backward. "What do you mean? What do you know?"

"Only what the cards have said. That sometimes you see him. Hear his voice. Even sense a little shadow walking close beside your own."

"How on…" I began then stopped my words when I realised that my eyes were prickling with tears. "How have you seen so much?"

Crowe's smile grew wider and a shade less sad. "Perhaps because the only possible explanation is that I have spoken to you, ever since our first encounter, nothing but the truth. That I am just what I appear to be and that the cards are exactly what I claim that they are. That I have a gift. That you were meant to meet me, meant to come here today and meant to assist me in what lies before us."

In that instant I understood that I had begun, against all better judgement and my lifelong commitment to rationalism, to believe in Mr Hubert Crowe.

As I spoke again, was it my imagination that I heard by my side, the thoughtful scuffle of childish boots? Surely, surely it was. "And what is it, then, that lies before us, Mr Crowe?"

"Great work," he said and his smile became a wide grin. "The very greatest."

XII

I wish I had time now to detail in full the sixteen months that followed. Yet my suspicion is that events are still moving swiftly – that there is much that has yet to befall us – and I dare not run the risk of not saying all I have to say of the horrors of Crispin Rye and of the man who lived there. So I must be quicker than I might ideally have wanted.

To understand how Mr Crowe and I came to find ourselves in the situation which currently bedevils us, you need to have at least a survey of what took place for the two of us between the finding of the Olney boy and our subsequent interview, and those dreadful events which I am shortly to relate.

In brief, our acquaintanceship became an association which deepened over time into friendship. This, I have no doubt, was a rarity for us both.

I grew to enjoy his company and he mine, over occasional meals and modest glasses of wine. We would speak of family, our educations and politics. The strange side of his life did not come up between us with any regularity, at least at first. There were, however, certain interviews and even some of what you might call investigations on which I accompanied him.

I have of late often had cause to wonder to what degree I truly believed in my friend's supposed abilities, in the odd, disquieting mystique of his cards. Nothing ever came as close to persuading me as had his words about the infant who would have been my brother, though there were a number of incidents which did the same: certain objects found, an adultery confirmed and – in the case of a member of Parliament – an election predicted correctly.

Yet there was nothing for which I could altogether reach to set aside the reality of the world as I had until then understood it. Did I merely indulge my friend? Ought I to have done more to challenge him?

Maybe I should have and perhaps the bill for my negligence is now becoming due.

There is perhaps just one thing I should set down before I continue – the case against Mr Crowe.

I was stopped last year shortly before Christmas, coming out of a meeting of the Committee, by a fleshy man with a stoop, in a dark hat, who gripped my arm, leant close to me and said: "You a friend of Hubert Crowe?" There was the smell of liquor on his breath.

I said that I was, and he sniffed at my confirmation.

"Better watch yourself, then," he said. "Man's a bloody fraud. Take it from one who knows."

He turned away at this and lurched into the bustling street.

"And what is your name, sir?" I called out, my tone, I dare say, a somewhat prissy one, as occurs when I am nervous.

"Jefferies!" he called back, over his shoulder. "Mr Connor Jefferies. Ask your friend about me!"

And then he was gone.

When I challenged Crowe later about the man, he would say only that the fellow had visited him and asked a particular question about his parentage. "He did not care for the answer that the cards provided," was all that he would say. Crowe always had some notion of professional discretion, I think, like a doctor or a priest.

On any more than this, my friend would not be drawn and so I let it lie. You may wonder at my decision. The reason for it is not a noble one or even one that is worthy even of note.

It is simply this: it had taken the arrival of Mr Crowe to make plain to me the depth and substance of my loneliness. Perhaps the Jefferies case represented a loose thread on which I should have pulled. Yet I did not. I did not care to. And it may be far too late now to know for sure.

XIII

The true nightmare began on August 15th, 1850.

London was hot and all its people were in a state of discomfort. The city is not one that does well in the heat. Even New York, in my view, makes a better fist of it. The streets were stinking and vile. The place was stewing horribly. Cool air was nowhere to be found, either inside or out.

I had worked hard all day but I was restless and ill at ease. I was pleased then to receive a note from Hubert Crowe, delivered by an urchin shortly before six o'clock. It read: "Something very strange has been made apparent to me. Might you be persuaded to attend?"

This was all that was needed. Trapped in my stifling set of rooms, I was more than ready to go to him.

It was in a state of stoic suffering, then, that I took myself to Pilate Court and to the residence, which I had come to know well, of Hubert Crowe.

He was seated in the Divination Room at the little table. Three cards were set out before him. By his side was a copy of that morning's edition of *The Times*, open at a page that was thick with lines of advertisement. One of these had been circled with a flourish.

"Good evening," said Crowe.

I said hello and added: "You summoned me?"

"Great work," he said, without looking up. "Do you remember when I said that to you?"

I said, of course, that I did.

"I expect you've been wondering exactly when the work in question might arrive?"

"Possibly," I replied. "Though I simply enjoy your company, as you know." The compliment went by unremarked.

I took a seat beside him. "I guess I ought to know the form by now. What's the reading to be about today?"

"I have asked the cards, Mr Malone, a very particular question concerning the future. And this is their reply. See for yourself," said Crowe, before touching each of the cards in turn. "The first of these is: A Rending of the Veil..." This card depicted a shroud, torn and tattered, fluttering from the end of a spear. "This second is The Giant's Shadow." Here I saw, upon a patch of vivid green grass, the grey outline of some distant lumbering titan. "Aha! And here is the most troubling and dangerous of them all, in the space accorded to the future: The Tiger Springs." This third card depicted a big cat of the jungle leaping out of the undergrowth, fangs bared and claws outstretched.

I frowned. "What does it mean?"

Still Crowe did not face me. "The Tiger is indicative of some imminent assault upon one's mental faculties. In the worst of cases, it can point to outright lunacy."

"Your mind is robust, I should have thought."

Crowe waved away the remark. "The cards do not lie. At least, not to me. The Tiger is coming."

"Then let it come," I said. "Do you have any notion as to what might be the context for its arrival?"

"Here." Crowe passed me up the newspaper with its solitary ringed advertisement. "See this."

I read what was printed there.

> FOR SALE: Country house – Fieldwick Hall – of splendid isolation and antiquity. East of England. Close to woodland and open fields. Sea some twenty miles hence. Apply to the Revd. C W Leigh-Stanley, Parish of Crispin Rye, Norfolk.

"What do you think of it?" Crowe asked.

"Not a great deal," I said. "It's some crumbling old manse, surely, which has no heirs or anybody to care for it. Most likely, the place is falling apart or else some local man would have bought it up by now and there would be no need for a London newspaper."

Crowe peered at me. "But you can see nothing else? You can sense nothing else?"

"Not I," I said. "Though I expect you can perceive the sinister?"

He paused. His words were melodramatic, but his manner, as ever, was even and calm.

"Something dreadful has happened there. On that site. In this… Crispin Rye. Some crossing of boundaries which ought not to have been traversed."

"How do you know this?"

Crowe sniffed as though his cards required no further explanation. "There has been a breach," he said, more to himself, I think, than to me. "And I have to see it for myself. I have to find out just what has happened there."

"So," I said, feeling a little dazed from the heat, "you want to go to the county of Norfolk? I have never been myself."

His gaze was direct. "I want to go to Norfolk, yes, and to the village to see Fieldwick Hall for myself."

"Will it be cooler there?" I asked.

"It's certainly possible," said Crowe, "though I can make no guarantees."

"Are you sure?" I asked, feeling an unexpected clamminess against my skin. "Are you quite sure that this place is worth seeing? That anything of interest has ever happened there at all?"

"Malone," said Crowe. "I have never felt the call of a place so strongly nor felt with such potency that some law of nature has been broken. But if you doubt me. If you wish to remain alone in London then, please... be my guest."

XIV

The choice was not a difficult one, not then. We went by rail and it was a pleasant thing at first to escape the city, to watch its dark towers fade away and be replaced by wide fields of green and patches of flourishing woodland.

When we had left London completely and the train was surrounded on both sides by countryside, Crowe leaned forwards and said: "I am very thankful, you know."

He had been largely silent for much of the journey until then and had even drifted briefly into sleep when we were joined temporarily in the carriage by an old man with a great many suitcases who departed at Colchester.

"Not at all," I said, thinking that he referred to my purchase of the tickets.

"No, I mean for coming with me."

Again, I simply shrugged. "My pleasure."

"Even so..." Crowe said. "This time it feels... significant, don't you think?"

"I'm not sure," I said.

"You'll see," is all that was said then by Crowe.

A brief exchange of smiles then as the train thundered on, further and further from civilisation and into the East. It seemed almost an act of defiance – the shining newness of the track and the engines, against a landscape which had, according to the history books, all but defeated the Romans.

I must beware of casting too large a retrospective shadow over that journey. I cannot pretend that I felt any particular presentiment of disaster, in fact, quite the opposite as our conversation roamed happily over the terrain of our past association.

I am also unable to recollect no sign of the discord between us that was soon to emerge.

At length, we reached the station at Thorpe, near to the city of Norwich. From here we hired a dog cart and a groom to take us deeper into the countryside. We caught but a glimpse of the city – the great spire of its cathedral – and then we were away, past flatlands and through dense forest, and we felt the same feeling creep over us both, a sense of growing isolation.

Several times I found myself examining the somewhat unattractive face of my friend as the gig lurched to and fro over the uneven ground. There was a look in his eyes for which I did not care, a glimmering of excitement which did not match our journey or our bleak surroundings at all. We arrived eventually in the village of Crispin Rye just as it was beginning to get dark. How dearly do I wish now that we had found the courage to turn back.

XV

Before my association with Mr Crowe I had never been a superstitious man. As his friend, I hope that I have maintained this air of sceptical scientism and it was in this spirit that I looked upon Fieldwick Hall at Crispin Rye.

We had passed first through the village itself, which seemed a quiet enough place – picturesque in its way but not without a certain kind of watchfulness. It boasted a small church and a single inn. A shop. A few dwelling-places. It seemed to laze and dream in the dusk. I was to become quite intimate with the place before long and though I'm not sure that my subsequent discoveries have not now tinted my first view of it with a wash of crimson, I do think that, even then, that village seemed somehow to be holding its breath.

Fieldwick Hall itself was a good mile beyond the village, in a state of splendid solitude. Our coachman left us at the end of a long driveway and we walked together down towards the house, both a little nervous now and full of obscure anticipation. Set amongst green acres, there were fields to the north and a patch of woodland to the west. The village lay to the south and to the east was only countryside and narrow roads.

In purely architectural terms there was nothing to render the place remarkable. Almost two centuries old, there was, however, both damage and a palpable air of dereliction. It looked careworn and dilapidated and there was considerable evidence that there had been, not too long ago, a fire. There were also a series of outbuildings visible, all of which looked sad and half-abandoned.

The atmosphere was a melancholy one. It had an untended

look, though I felt nothing more sinister there than that. Yet Crowe evidently saw more.

"How fascinating," he said as we stood side by side and looked up at the edifice together for the first time. "Can you feel it? Something like a... trembling in the air? Like a sound just out of range?"

I said that I was able to hear none of these things.

"You think that I'm being fanciful?"

I was about to say that this judgement would not always, in his case, be altogether unjust when the great door to the Hall opened and a man of about sixty emerged – tall, lean, bony and stooped – who I took at first to be simply the agent who had agreed to meet us here. It soon became clear, however, that he played a larger role than that in this part of the world for he wore the garb of a country priest.

"Gentlemen, welcome! Welcome to Fieldwick Hall." He extended his right hand. With a jolt of disgust, I saw that his left hand was missing two fingers. "I'm the Reverend Leigh-Stanley."

We introduced ourselves in turn.

This done, the priest suggested: "I thought you would want to see something of the interior. The light is fading now. I trust you have accommodation arranged for the night?"

I said that we had and named the village inn.

"The Mariner's Rest? You could do worse than that. Best, I think, to see the rest of the grounds in daylight. But for now, let me show you inside. I can tell you a little of the history of the place. The price is very reasonable, I think, and the owner has given me full authority to conduct any and all negotiations."

"Oh?" I said. "And where exactly is the owner at present?"

The face of the priest was imperturbable. "He is engaged elsewhere. He has many responsibilities. And as I say, I am licensed to stand in his place."

A look which I had come to know well settled now over the features of my friend, a kind of weird and unexpected wisdom. "He is confined," he said.

Leigh-Stanley looked oddly at him. "Yes..." he began, then seemed to staunch his own words. "Well, he is a very private man, Mr Crowe. I can tell you that much. But he is very keen to see affairs dealt with promptly and despatched in full. Now then, shall we go inside?"

He turned, without awaiting our response, and walked towards the entrance. Crowe and I followed, not speaking.

A moment later and we were all within that wretched house and the door was closed behind us and, to all intents and purposes, my friend was damned.

XVI

In the days that have followed our entrance into Fieldwick Hall I have thought often of what we saw, of how it gripped and fascinated poor Crowe. Looking back now, it seems as though we walked into an expertly baited trap. As to who, or what, had set it and to what purpose I am yet to fully understand.

Back then I felt nothing save for a vague unease. Certainly, there was nothing that I could have done to alter the result in any way or to cool the enthusiasm of my associate. This, at least, is what I have taken to telling myself when I wake in clammy fretfulness in the watches of the night.

The interior was large and had once been as grand a place as you might find in so distant and isolated a village. Only three or four of the chambers showed any recent sign of habitation, and from certain signs I took one of these people to have been a child. There was a kind of makeshift schoolroom which looked well-used. There were toys and a small bedroom. There were scribblings upon the wall.

The servants' quarters were extensive but seemed to have descended into utter neglect. The place looked as though it had been taken over by trespassers for all that the Reverend Leigh-Stanley assured us that the mysterious absent owner was a man of means and standing.

I asked again for this man's name but the old priest just waved aside the question. He did the same when I enquired as to the reason for the condition of the Hall. As we walked through the house in the gathering gloom, through its wood-panelled hallways, through its dining rooms and studies, I could certainly see how it might still be made very comfortable for a man with a modest fortune and squirearchical ambitions, though I could not for the life of me see why Crowe was so excited by the prospect.

That is, until we reached a chamber which Leigh-Stanley informed us, had once been the ballroom, the largest and grandest room by far in all that edifice and the one which now troubles me the most.

It was a big space, grander than the tumbledown air of the rest of the mansion might have suggested, and I could see it had once been very fine indeed, in the far-off days, perhaps, of the old century.

Yet it wore a dismal face.

Fire had broken out there in recent times, just as it had on the exterior of the building, though mercifully this conflagration had not spread beyond the door. There were scorch marks all along the north and east walls and many other signs of devastation.

Some vague repair work had been conducted but no serious effort had been made to hide the fact that a mighty crisis had only narrowly been averted. It seemed to me something of a miracle given the obvious intensity of the blaze that it had not brought the whole Hall down with it.

"Reverend?" I asked, meaning to be plain-speaking. "What exactly happened here?"

The Reverend Leigh-Stanley wore a look of something like embarrassment. He rocked on his heels and would not meet my gaze. "There was an accident," he said. "It was unfortunate, yes... but these things do happen. There is still so much that could be done to restore it. It is a question only of time and of money... of money and of time..."

As he spoke, my eyes drifted about the room and I could not help but linger on certain troubling potholes and indentations on the floor as though some great weight had been dropped from a height on it.

"But all this damage," I said, "it's not all caused by fire. Not by any means."

A pained expression was evident upon the angular face of the priest. "Well..." he began, though he was not to complete his sentence for my friend, Mr Crowe, at once broke in.

"There was a piercing..." he said, and his gaze was not on us or on anything there but was rather fixed into the middle distance. "A piercing of the world and what lies beyond."

I was well accustomed to such pronouncements, though the vicar was not. I was about to apologise to him but then I saw the most extraordinary expression cross Leigh-Stanley's face. It was something like fear, but not only that. It was edged with something close to panic.

"Should not the dead stay dead?" asked Crowe, his delivery slower than normal, a recognisable effect of that trance-like state which he was now fast approaching. His question seemed to puzzle even him, as though he was unsure of the answer.

Leigh-Stanley, meanwhile, seemed to have mastered himself. His smile restored, he said: "Now was there anything else that you gentlemen wished to see? Or shall we conclude our viewing for today?"

XVII

We were taken to the inn by the Reverend Leigh-Stanley in his gig. Crowe kept up a stream of questions to which the priest could provide only answers of increasing evasiveness. He seemed himself now to be deeply uncomfortable even in having shown us the property. The thought flitted across my mind that he was doing this only reluctantly and under some unseen pressure.

The inn itself was small and too hot and filled with unhealthy rustics. Over supper, Crowe spoke to me with an animation and excitement which I had not observed in him for months. His conversation was all of the possibilities of Fieldwick Hall as he saw it. He was oblivious to the dark looks and muttered expressions of irritation from the local men by whom we were surrounded.

"But what are you going to do with it?" I asked at last, in some exasperation.

"Oh, I should have thought that was obvious. I mean to buy it, repair it and to live in it."

"Why in the name of the good Lord would you want to do a thing like that?"

"To see if I can understand what was done in that place. The fissure that was created between the world of the living and the world of the dead."

"You're still convinced that something happened there?"

Behind us, at the bar, some simmering argument about livestock seemed to be about to grow more severe. Crowe seemed oblivious to it all.

"Aren't you?" he asked.

By this time, my head was turned for I feared the dispute between the two farming gentlemen was threatening to burst the banks of polite debate altogether.

Crowe took quiet umbrage at my distraction.

"Come now," he said as I returned my attention to our little table and away from the disputatious cattlemen. "Haven't you seen enough yet? Haven't you witnessed enough with me to trust in my abilities?" He took a single, shallow breath. "To believe in me?"

I hesitated and he saw my moment of hesitation.

"I see," was all that he said as behind us I heard the sound of the first punch being thrown.

Some considerable chaos ensued while the two opponents were escorted by force from the premises. As a spectacle it was absorbing, though my friend seemed scarcely to notice, but kept on chewing his food till the hubbub had subsided.

He wore a look by then of interrogation which I found somewhat irritating.

"There is certainly something odd about the house," I admitted. "Odd about the old priest too. Odd about…" I gestured discreetly around me "…all of this. But if you truly feel such a compulsion, why can you not simply investigate the place? Rather than buying it outright?"

"On that point," Crowe replied evenly, "the estate has been very clear. The building and its grounds are strictly private. No scholars of any kind are permitted to enter it. Our choices are to buy the place or else to leave behind us the most queerly troubling mystery I've ever encountered."

I delivered a cold truth then. Meant to calm him, it succeeded merely in exacerbating his mood. "But you can't possibly afford it."

Crowe gave me a look of quick cunning. "No," he said. "But you can."

XVIII

I do not wish to dwell on the row which then ensued between Mr Hubert Crowe and I. We had disagreed on little in our association but the argument which developed between us that night was tremendous.

Ugly words were issued from both sides. Secret views were expressed and unkind judgements were passed. He accused me of never truly understanding his work or of appreciating its potential. I, in turn, and now somewhat to my shame, said that his chief interest in me was financial and that I had finally ceased to wish to indulge his fancies at the cost of my own far from infinite fortune.

So badly, in fact, did things go between us that I said I wished to have nothing more to do with him, a suggestion to which he violently assented. It was a most inelegant business and we went to our rooms on the very worst of terms. I have noted since that Crispin Rye and its surrounding region would seem to be the kind of place where tempers fray more easily than they do elsewhere.

My sleep was a fitful thing, much interrupted by nightmares. I saw in them a figure moving, a very tall dark man, trapped in mud beneath the ground. He was struggling against the pull of it but he was reluctant also, as if a part of him wished to be lost beneath the surface forever.

And I saw two other things also — two of Crowe's damned cards dancing before me, as much an absurd sight as one comprised of menace. I saw the Tiger about to spring and I saw that hideous toad creature, the demon whom Crowe had once called Antenar.

I woke to an empty room just before the dawn. All was silence. I took a few long deep breaths to soothe my restless imagination and I returned myself to sleep.

XIX

When I woke in the morning I found Crowe's room empty and the man himself flown. He had paid for precisely one half of the tariff. The landlord of The Mariner's Rest told me only that my friend had risen early and declared his intention to go back to London.

"What was his mood?" I asked.

The publican – a pale, thoughtful man who seemed oddly ill-suited to his profession – seemed noncommittal. "Well enough," he said. "Happy and eager to be off." I must have looked confused at this for the fellow added, as if to reassure me: "Though I have to say, I was glad to see the back of him. Not for my sake, you understand, sir, but for his."

"Oh? Now, what do you mean by that?"

"It was the house, sir... Fieldwick Hall. A man like your friend rooting about in a place like that... Why, no good can come of it."

"What makes you say so?"

"You've not heard the stories about the place, sir?"

"There are stories about the Hall?"

"Many stories, sir. And much in the way of facts too." His stolid expression made it clear that he meant to relate not a one of them. "Let's just say, sir, between the two of us, that the more distance your friend can put between him and Fieldwick Hall, the better for his own sake... his own sanity... his own..." The landlord hesitated.

I prompted him. "Yes?"

"His own soul, sir," he said and so ended our last conversation to date.

XX

After this weird exchange, I did a thing which I believe you'll think most queer, and even somewhat foolish. I went back to the property that was for sale to see it again for myself. My friend, after all, had returned to London, where I sorely hoped, he might "cool down" soon enough. It was over him that the house had woven its strange spell and not over me. Or so, at least, I said to myself.

Seeing it now, written down as clear as that, I can see the folly of my words.

I walked alone through the village and out to its furthest extremity quite happily in the daylight.

There was nothing especially sinister in that little conurbation though I was aware, on some animal level as folk cast their gazes down at my approach and shuttered their windows too hastily, that it was a place of unspoken secrets. Yet what small community is not?

Had I not quarrelled so badly with Crowe and if my concern had not been so great for him the walk might even have been a pleasant one. When I reached the Hall, I found its doors all locked and no sign of the priest from the day before.

And as for Fieldwick Hall itself? In the cool country light of the morning with green fields stretching away on one side of it, and the patch of woodland to the west, it seemed as tranquil a place as I have ever seen, and I wondered at the exaggerations of our behaviour only hours before.

Crowe was (I hope still is) a singular man with plentiful gifts who often in my presence has been fearless, yet he is capable also of something like hysteria. As I gazed at the high walls and cracked windows of the place and took in its air of scorched dilapidation I wondered if we had not just imagined much of what had so excited us.

Now, I admit freely that my relationship with my Creator is a complicated thing but I found myself then in that soft and rustic spot suddenly compelled to pray, for guidance and for aid. It was the first time I had done so in years, and I have not attempted to do so since. Beside the Hall, I sank down into the long grass and closed my eyes, only to become, almost at once, uncomfortably and pricklingly aware that I was being watched.

I opened my eyes and got quickly to my feet. Whirling around, I looked at the house and then back in the direction of the village.

Towards the west a man was watching me from the line of trees. For a long moment, we looked at one another. He was squat, haggard, running to fat; wild-looking indeed in that context, standing in silhouette against oak and ash.

I raised a hand. The stranger did not respond, remaining instead dead still.

Under an influence I could not explain, I began to walk towards him, away from the Hall and towards the woodland, meaning to speak to the visitor, man to man.

Seeing my approach, he turned and ran.

I have never been anything like an athlete. At school, I always rather despised the boyish cult of sportsmanship. Yet I did not need to be an expert to win this particular race. My opponent was in poor condition and he floundered hopelessly ahead of me through the trees. Yet for a while the chase was on between us. I pushed myself onwards and I soon felt my body complain at the exertion. Yet my quarry was in a worse state.

He was also moderately inebriated. He stumbled over a tree root or a fallen branch, and tumbled, face-first, into foliage.

Panting, I reached his side.

"Who are you?" I asked.

The surly fellow rolled with difficulty onto his back and glared up at me.

"Well?" I asked.

"Name's Tebb."

This conveyed nothing whatever to me and I told him so. He gestured curtly towards the Hall.

"Used to work in there," he said. "At Fieldwick."

"Is that right? Well, you don't work there now. The place is up for sale."

He grinned. "Still like to keep an eye on it."

"Why?"

He grunted. "The Hall... it takes a hold on you." At these words, a bird, startled, rose noisily into the sky.

"What do you mean?"

"It... calls out to you."

"Is that so?"

While he had been speaking, Tebb began to rise in laborious stages to his feet. I fear I offered him no assistance.

At last, he stood opposite me, red-faced and indignant. "Who are you anyways? You come to buy the Hall?"

"Now, is that a thing you would recommend?"

He gave me a sly look. "Depends if it's called you..."

"You keep saying such things. But what do you mean?"

Tebb looked back at the house again, as though he could not quite stop himself. "Place speaks to a particular kind of man. The first Squire of the place, back in the days of foundation; a man in my grandpa's day who lost his head; the man who owns it now... And one other."

I had many questions but in the moment I asked only one. "Who?"

A dreamy, faraway look came over his stolid features. "A man who came from Geneva… a doctor…"

"What?"

Tebb tried to muster up some dignity. He brushed down his shoulders, drew in a breath and raised himself to his full height. I wondered where he lived and if, as he appeared, he were not simply a gentleman of the road.

"Shouldn't say more, sir. Shouldn't say more."

He turned and hurried away, taking more quick glances as he went at the edifice. I let him go without further interview. His presence was most distasteful to me. He had about him a disagreeable odour and, as you know, I cannot abide proximity.

XXI

Having by now had my fill of signs and portents, of hints and whispered rumours, I returned to London and settled back into my ordinary life. The Assembly took up a deal of my time and I did my utmost to exhaust myself in the daytime so as not to be disturbed at night by bad dreams.

I tried not to think or to concern myself unduly with Mr Crowe. Ours was ever a complicated friendship. I believed then that the best course of action would be to leave him to his own devices.

Besides, I had my own pride.

Still, three days went by and then four and then five, and I found myself on the cusp of setting aside our quarrel and seeking him out, to satisfy myself as to his well-being.

Then on the morning of the sixth day — August 23rd — he arrived without warning in my own rooms, filled with seeming good cheer and bonhomie, and evidently choosing to pretend that our harsh exchange of words had never happened. If I had any sentiments on the matter, I kept them to myself.

"You seem in high spirits," I said, once Mrs Armitage had shown him up and left us. The Southwark Prophet was seated opposite me in an armchair.

"Oh, well that is because I have news, Malone. Truly excellent news."

It concerned me afresh to find him in such a mood for he was ever a creature of extremes.

"And what is your news?"

"You recall the house at Crispin Rye? Fieldwick Hall?" He said this with a kind of vague, studied insouciance which struck me as absurd.

"Of course I do."

"I have news of two developments related to that singular edifice."

I drew in a careful breath. "Go on then."

"Well, the first, though not necessarily the most interesting, is that I have managed to buy the Hall."

"How?"

He looked at me directly. "I have been busy raising funds."

"I don't understand."

"I have helped many people over the years. Long before I met you. And a good many of them remain grateful. And eager to help."

"Loans?" I asked. "Or gifts?"

"A little of both and, I will grant you, it has taken some

doing. Yet it has been done. And so here we are. I have instructed a lawyer to arrange matters with the Reverend Leigh-Stanley. There are expected to be no obstacles and the property should become mine by the end of the month."

"My God… are you sure, Hubert? Are you absolutely sure?"

"It's a special place. I think you sensed that."

"Special, yes. But to whom? To what kinds of men?"

Crowe grinned then, a child's giddy smile at the promise of some unexpected treat. "Well, yes, indeed and that brings me to my secondary piece of good news."

As he spoke, I felt the beginnings of a bad headache. "And what is that?"

"I've found the man who owned the Hall before me. The seller! Oh, Leigh-Stanley tried to keep it from me, to disguise the fellow's name and cover up his tracks… but I've found him all right. Yes, I've hunted him down."

"Oh? And who is he? Where is he?"

"His name is Nathaniel Greene."

Somewhere, dimly, the name seemed familiar. An expert in the folklore of London but something else besides…

"And as to where he is, why, let me show you." Crowe got hastily to his feet. "I'll whistle up a cab and we can see him forthwith. He's waiting for us. We've corresponded. He's promised to tell me everything. Make a clean breast of it." Crowe winked at me. "Give us his… confession."

"Crowe, for God's sake," I began, meaning to demand that he explain himself but he was already halfway out of the room by then and moving at speed down the stairs.

It will not surprise you by now to learn that I followed.

XXII

On the short journey that ensued, Crowe would answer not a single one of my questions but just grinned on in that new, maddening way of his.

He looked out at the grime of the city. It was as though he was not seeing it as it was, but rather looking through it to some other, hidden space beyond.

As the cab rattled through the filthy, stinking streets, my headache grew acute. I knew, of course, that something was terribly wrong though I did not yet appreciate the extent of it.

Gradually, our destination became plain. I guessed at the truth a few minutes before we arrived.

"Crowe?" I asked with (I don't doubt) an edge of anger to my voice. "Is this man incarcerated?"

"I always knew he was confined. Don't you remember? When we were at the Hall? I saw it." As he spoke, the great and terrible outline of Newgate prison hove with bleak inevitability into view. You have, perhaps, seen this place for yourself? A dark and awful citadel whose stones speak of death and of the recesses of despair. It is, as you will surely know, not only a place of imprisonment but also one of execution.

"What has this man done?" I asked. "To be sentenced here?"

The cab was drawing nearer to the wretched portal of the gaol. At our approach, even Crowe had the good grace to drop from his lips that impertinent smile.

"I do believe," he said, "that the gentleman in question, the former owner of Fieldwick Hall, murdered his wife." For a dreadful second, that grin returned to the surface. "Though, as he will shortly endeavour to explain, he had his reasons. Let us hope he is swift for he is to hang in five days time."

At the callousness of his words, my headache seemed to double in strength. By the time that we reached the gate and alighted, it was a potent distraction indeed. Much that followed remains seared on my memory but the particulars of how we came to step down from our transport, passed through the gate and were led, by some unsmiling gaoler, through the echoing corridors of that appalling citadel, seem now to be elusive to me.

I remember the shrieks of the incarcerated, the hopeless wailing and gnashing of teeth. Yet stronger than that is how simple it all was, with what dread ease we were shepherded to the cell of Nathaniel Greene. I must have said something of the sort to my companion for Crowe turned to me and said: "I told you... there are a lot of men in London who were grateful to me. Before this week, I doubt that I've ever called in so much as a single favour."

And then we reached it: a cell of solitary confinement. Our guide unlocked the door and bade us enter. The next thing that I knew, Mr Crowe and I were standing in a gloomy, malodorous place, as vile a dungeon as one could imagine. The door behind us was slammed and bolted.

To my surprise, I saw that three chairs had been arranged, set in a rough triangle. Out of the shadows stepped a man in his middle years, dark-haired and portly, with the eyes of an intelligent sensualist. He moved slowly, and with a limp. There was a small white scar on his forehead.

"You are Mr Crowe?" he said, his soft and sombre voice an incongruous thing in that spot of damnation.

"I am," said my friend.

"You came, then?"

"I said that I would. This is my friend from the Americas, Mr Malone."

The prisoner, Nathaniel Greene, looked over at me distractedly. "Please, gentlemen, both of you sit down. I fear that I can offer you no refreshment."

"It scarcely matters," said Crowe, sitting eagerly in his chair and beckoning for me to do the same. My head seemed now to pulse with rising discomfort. I sat down, dazed, hot, afraid.

"Are you sure, gentlemen," said Nathaniel Greene, as he settled into the third chair, "that you wish to know? The whole truth? About what has brought me here? About the death of my wife and the Genevese physician? About the true nature of the Hall at Crispin Rye?"

"We would like nothing more," said Crowe, his eyes burning with an unstaunched curiosity.

"Very well," said the convict. "Then, please, permit me to begin."

PART THREE

THE CONFESSION OF NATHANIEL GREENE*

---

* It is my supposition that this portion of the text represents a kind of remembered transcript by Jesse Malone. As such, I cannot vouch for its absolute accuracy.

- 1 -
SUNDRY PREFATORY MATTERS

For the whole of my life I have striven, above all other things, to be honest, faithful and true. In each of these ambitions I have failed and it is that utter moral dereliction which has led me now to this most dreadful of passes, unto the very shadow of the noose.

There is, however, one other besides myself upon whom I can in part blame my present predicament – namely that monstrous Genevese physician whose very arrival set in motion the ruination of all I once held dear.

Yet I wish it to be understood by you both, gentlemen, and to be placed absolutely upon record, that I accept the great majority of the fault as being mine and mine alone. I am the chief architect of my own destruction. I am most assuredly guilty – guilty of much folly, guilty of waywardness and infidelity, and guilty, above all, of that crime for which I have been sentenced. Yes, gentlemen, I did indeed carry out the killing of my wife. It was in some respects an act born of mercy and I wish that there had been another way, but I cannot in good conscience deny the justice of my arrest and incarceration.

So, please, my friends, before the shadow descends, permit me to explain everything in full. We must be swift for the clock is working hard against us. Yet I shall not stint on detail for it is in certain particulars where the true nature of that evil which I permitted to overtake me may most plainly be spied.

- 2 -
THE STRANGER IN THE SNOW

On the day when the stranger came first to our home, trailing clouds of wickedness in his wake, I was absent and my wife was alone, vulnerable and unguarded.

You have seen the Hall at Crispin Rye, more recently than I, so you will doubtless recall the size of the place, its loneliness and utter isolation. You may recall its echoing passageways, its plentiful rooms — never one of them of the same proportions as any other! — as well as those many, half-abandoned outbuildings which are dotted about the main structure. You may recall also the wild flatlands that lie to the east of the property, the fields that are to the north and that little patch of sylvan woodland which lies to the west. You will remember how the village of Crispin Rye itself is a full mile distant to the south. It is a house, then, of splendid and terrible seclusion. Indeed, these are the chief reasons why I chose it.

I bought the place in the spring of 1840, meaning to spend my time there upon the completion of a book in which I could explore the secret folklore of London. Alice, my wife at that time of but four years, had most definite hopes of her own, of a child and a growing family.

Yet in the time that had elapsed since the purchase, our ambitions had been thwarted. My own work I had neglected. I had written little of my book. It is instead these words — this confession — which must act instead as my legacy.

Alice blamed me for our lack of success in the production of what one might call an heir. She cursed me for taking her to this lonely spot when I had, in the days of our courtship, presented myself as being a creature of the city.

"You have not been fair to me," she would say. "You have not been honest. And you have brought me nothing but grief, Nathaniel."

Her sorrow was without question though there was little I could do to staunch it. If she should seem to you gentlemen to be presented in this account of mine as a mere shrew then you should know that her actions were grounded, from the first, in pain.

My story begins in earnest on January 15th, 1843. It was dusk, the light was fading and Alice was all alone. We had once had a larger staff of domestics but, due to local rumours, we had encountered much trouble in retaining them and by this time we had just two remaining servants – Mr and Mrs Tebb, a sullen and an idle couple in their middle years who seemed nonetheless to be devoted to one another.

There were more duties, of course, than could possibly be done by this pair and so, even then at this early stage, the house and all that surrounded it had begun to slip towards decay. Both of the Tebbs were absent that afternoon, having made a trip to Wymondham to see her sister's family. They were to stay overnight and to return late the following day. They made of us so few requests (for all their surly demeanours) that I did not think this mild imposition could lightly be denied.

I am, sirs, no believer in providence or fate yet things could scarcely have been better prepared for *his* arrival and the circumstances made no more ideal for his entrance into our lives had they been laid out deliberately and set in place by some unseen engineer.

Alice told me later how it happened.

She was in the library, not reading but simply gazing from the window, looking west towards the line of narrow, leafless trees and into the dwindling light. As she watched, and rather in the manner of some old fairy tale, it began to snow, white speckles against the twilight. Then she glimpsed something else. She said to me once that there was something almost painterly in the scene. She saw a figure step softly from the woodland, gazing with apparent intensity of purpose in the direction of the Hall.

Alice claimed that she did not understand her motivation for what she did then, but she raised her hand first in greeting and then, more awfully, in a gesture of beckoning. The stranger seemed somehow to see her — perhaps, of course, it was merely her silhouette — and he began to stalk deliberately towards the house.

As he did so, my wife perceived him more clearly: a lean man of around seventy with close-cropped hair and an imperious set of features. He looked ragged, as though he had fallen on unhappy times, and his gait was stilted and uncertain as if he suffered from some long illness and had just stepped, at long last, from his sickbed.

He was dressed, she saw, all in white, a long garment that was tattered and torn. He looked like a soiled angel or else some Old Testament prophet transplanted to the countryside of England.

Closer came the man and closer still, moving away from the trees and towards our home as though it had always been his destination.

And as she watched him come nearer and nearer, my wife stood, motionless, and was filled up with what she called a dual emotion — profound disquiet mingled, she told me, with the most unexpected feeling of joy.

- 3 -
THE DRAPER'S WIDOW

You will be wondering, gentlemen, how precisely I might have been occupied at this moment, as my wife, alone in our dwelling-place, watched the white-clad stranger approach.

My location and, indeed, my occupation at what I take to have been the instant that my wife first saw the visitor is a source of great and everlasting shame to me.

Gentlemen, in the early days of our acquaintanceship and at the very outset of marriage, I did love my wife – I truly did – but whereas her nature was water and ice, mine is fire and lava. Such a mingling of spirits led inevitably to a cooling, first from passion into friendship and then, following our disappointments, from friendship into a kind of mutual tolerance.

You look askance at me, gentlemen. You wish me to explain? You wish me to tell you the precise nature of my sin? Women, sirs. Five in total over the years since we had first come to Crispin Rye. Elizabeth, Mary, Polly, Sarah and Eliza. And it was Eliza with whom I was sequestered that day – Eliza Smith, the widow of a draper who lived in a small cottage by the sea, in a town called Marlowe's Brook.

Though widowed, she was still young – fifteen years my junior. We had met the Christmas of the year before when I had conducted one of my philosophical perambulations along the shore.

Her eyes were bright and quick, and in spite of her considerable material disadvantages, she possessed a readier and a fuller smile than anyone else of my acquaintance.

I tell you these things, gentlemen, so that you might

understand that ours was a true relation and not simply base desire.

I see from your demeanours that you do not, perhaps, altogether believe me in this. Very well. Make any assumption that you will. Only I and the lady herself know the truth of the arrangement. One of us has already passed beyond the veil in dreadful circumstances and the other of us is set soon to join her.

You need know only this – that I was with her that afternoon as the light was fading and as the snow began to fall.

We were in her cottage, together and in secret, both a little in our cups and – no, gentlemen, I shall not flinch from it – we were in that warmest and most animal of states.

I am no believer, in ghosts and spirits, sir, at least I was not so once. Yet I have dwelled long upon the detail and I am in my own mind quite satisfied that the times were the same, of me with Eliza and of my wife with the stranger. In the midst of my pleasure, I felt a sudden, piercing sense of fear. It was not pain but rather a coldness in my blood and a trembling in my body – the echo, I now believe, of my wife's own emotion.

Suddenly afraid, I took myself away from my paramour and sunk into the far side of the bed.

"What is it?" asked Eliza, her kind brown eyes alight with concern. "Whatever ails you?"

I could not say. I could not form a single word. I gaped at her and it was not until moments later that I realised I was weeping.

- 4 -
VICTOR AT THE WINDOWPANE

My wife watched as the man crossed the half-dead grass before the house. It was, she said, a moment of complete silence. Even the Hall – often so noisy, so full of echoes and creaks – seemed to quieten, as though it too were watching the approach of the stranger with a combination of curiosity and wonder. The man seemed to stumble, then picked up his feet and came closer. She saw that he appeared to be struggling and that he was in a state of some distress. His face was beaded with the sweat of exertion. Still she did not move – unable, she said, to do anything more than bear witness – as he limped towards the window.

Once there, he paused, his arms hanging limply by his sides and the two of them observed one another as might a visitor to a menagerie gaze upon a creature in a cage (though, which was which I cannot say) until the man raised his hand in feeble greeting. My wife was about to do the same when the newcomer sank with sudden violence onto the ground and onto the snow which was by then starting to settle.

Alice was all motion. It was as though some spell had been broken. She thought to call for our servants only to remember that they were both away and so she hurried out of the room herself, down the long hallway which led to the outer door then off into the grounds beyond. The air was almost uncomfortably crisp. Her life had been for so long a sedentary and a mournful thing that it felt a shock to be asked by events to move at speed. Snow was in her eyes and the scene swam before her. Soon she reached the stranger who had not righted himself but who still lay sprawled upon the earth.

She drew nearer to him, concerned but wary. He turned his head at the sound of her footsteps.

He made a soft gurgling sound which she could not at first decipher.

"Who are you?" she said. "What has brought you here?"

The same soft gurgling as before.

She bent low towards him, one hand extended and she heard what he was trying, pleadingly, to say: "Help me... help me, help me, please..." His voice was flecked with some indeterminate European accent. "Help me... and I will give you... your heart's desire..."

Though weakly spoken, his every word was filled with dreadful conviction. My wife said in a dull, faraway voice, like that of a mesmerist's subject, "Very well."

She bent down further and helped him, trembling, to his feet and in the time that it took to perform that simple act of kindness we all of us were lost.

- 5 -
A WARNING

It seems to come upon many men of my age and station that having laboured since the days of their youth to build for themselves a sturdy and well-constructed life, they then set about the absolute destruction of it all.

Had my wife ever been confronted with unquestionable evidence of my infidelities, my existence would have been made a daily torment. She may even have considered more drastic, ruinous and, above all, costly steps.

These were the thoughts by which I was flooded as, having dried my eyes, I dressed as hurriedly as I was able on the far side of the bedroom. Eliza, still upon the bed and in an unblushing state, was observing my haste and indignity.

"Thought you was staying tonight," she said, not without a note of sulkiness. "Thought you meant to treat me nicely."

I began to apologise, a stream of ill-considered excuses, then stopped myself, turned to face her and said, with candour entire: "I have to go home. I have not the slightest notion as to why but I have to go back immediately."

She chewed her lower lip thoughtfully. "You felt something, then?"

"My dear, I felt many things," I began, hoping to recapture some of our old gaiety.

"No," she said and her tone was free now of pleading. "You felt a… reaching out?"

I said that I did and she nodded. "I have felt that before," she said. "Last week…"

"Yes?"

She hesitated. "I thought I saw my father."

"Your father?"

I knew that the gentleman in question (who was, of course, no gentleman, but rather a violent drinker of the coarsest and most unsavoury sort) had passed away at least a decade before. This could not, then, have been any natural encounter.

"What do you mean?"

"Last night when I was alone here, the day before you were due… I saw him watching me."

"Then you were dreaming."

"Not dreaming. I was awake."

"Come now, you know as well as I how porous are the territories between slumber and the waking world."

She pouted and, as if suddenly ashamed, pulled close to her the blankets on the bed. "I did not dream it," she said again, as though I were a fool for speaking as I had. This was a tone which she had hitherto been careful not to employ in my presence.

Hurriedly, I tied my cravat and pulled it tight, then set beside that tender lady.

"What is it?" I asked, permitting myself a note of humility. "What ails you?"

"I told you," she said. "I saw him. My father. He spoke to me."

I relented still further, deciding to humour her. "Perhaps such things are not altogether impossible. Sometimes perhaps, yes, maybe... There are things — and personages too — which appear to us as shades or echoes."

She frowned, as if trying to remember something which lay just beyond the scope of her recall. "And there was a warning," she said. "A warning — queer though I know it must sound — a warning for you, Nathaniel."

So rarely did she use my name that this detail alone aroused my concern. I had not found myself in such a mood for years, that sense of being all at once outpaced by events, of some shift in the order of things which I was powerless to affect. "What was it?" I asked, and that room, once so full for me of gentle comforts, seemed to be sunk then into shadow. "What did your father say?"

A most curious expression passed across her face, as of a cloud before the moon.

"He told you to kill the stranger in the snow."

- 6 -
OUR SECOND-BEST BED

I remember only a little of my journey home that night, save that it was dark and the rain was persistent, and the narrow country roads upon which I travelled were dim, oppressive things, framed alternately by wide, bleak fields and by glowering patches of woodland, the arms of empty trees outstretched against me as I thundered past.

If this sounds to you, gentlemen, as though it possessed the qualities of a nightmare then I dare say that the judgement would not be so very far wide of the mark. I am, I fear, a poor horseman at the best of times, uneasy with the animal and inexpert in matters of navigation. I would always prefer to be driven and, had my appointment been of any other sort, I would surely have asked for Mr Tebb to take me to the door of the draper's widow.

Yet one must remember to keep secrets from one's servants and, in this instance, from the Tebbs in particular for they nursed for my wife an odd and even sentimental loyalty which, so far as I could see, had never received the smallest encouragement or reciprocation.

That night I was almost thrown several times from the back of my steed. Twice, or even three times, I thought that I had taken altogether the wrong turn yet, somehow, I arrived home, intact and shortly after midnight, to find the house in absolute darkness with the exception of a single flickering source of light from the library.

Having stabled the horse, cursing Tebb anew as I did so for his absence, I stole into the lighted room, altogether uncertain as to what I would find there.

Without the servants, the Hall seemed even quieter and more still than usual though I think perhaps I sensed even then that it was not so very empty as all that. Alice sat alone, her face illumined by a candle's glow.

She sat, motionless, at my approach.

I cleared my throat a little too vigorously — a nervous habit that I cannot seem to curb whenever I face my wife for the first time immediately following a bout of the unfaithful.

I did this once, twice, three times, until I began to sound as though I had acquired some fresh affliction. There was nothing so very extraordinary in this — relations between my wife and I, having long since fallen into such stretches of dreadful silence — and I even began to wonder if I had not been overly fanciful in my fears and whether it was merely guilt and shame which had compelled me to return home, with the words of the widow reverberating in my imagination. Then my wife turned at last to face me and I knew that my concerns were not unfounded and that there was something very wrong indeed in our house for Alice had upon her lips a smile of great bliss, such as I had never seen there.

"Nathaniel," she said, and her voice was filled with wonder. "At last, someone has come to help us."

"What has happened?" I asked and she told me, more or less, what I have already described to you — the vision of the stranger at the window.

As soon as she had finished, her every word delivered in a kind of hushed reverence, I went to the chamber in which he had been laid, wishing to see this visitor for myself and to confirm that he was real and not some wishful figment of my wife's.

Yes there he was, that old, lean, physician, sleeping in our second-best bed for all the world as though he owned it.

He had a pale, thoughtful face, a little sunken due to age and increasing frailty but still with the marks of those good looks which he must have had in his youth. His breathing was shallow but regular and he seemed even then to be becoming something better and stronger than that near-spectral figure who had emerged hours before from amid the trees.

"But who is he?" I asked. "Where does he come from? What does he want?"

Alice was beside me. She touched my left shoulder, glancingly. "His name is Victor Frankenstein. All of those other things will be revealed to us in time."

"But there are authorities…" I said. "Charities. Hostels for the poor. The workhouse in Gressenhall."

"No," she said, and her voice was firmer. "He stays here with us."

"Alice…"

Her eyes flashed fire. "No. What do I ask of you? Nothing. Nothing at all. So let me take this."

I looked back at the stranger in the bed. In that unguarded moment, he had to him a vulnerability which I was never again to witness.

"For a night or two," I said. "No more than that. There must be people searching for him. His family."

"Thank you," Alice said. "Let us see how he fares in the morning. Rest now."

She turned and went away to her room. I stayed an instant more and watched the visitor.

Oh, how often have I wondered since how different so

many things might now be if only I had found the courage to place upon his face a cushion and, in the space of a few merciful minutes, taken away his life!

- 7 -
THE FIRST MORNING

I was awoken the following morning by sounds which had not been heard in that house for many years. The first of the noises was laughter; the second, somehow still more unexpected, was that of a pleasant tenor voice, lifted high in song. The words and melody were unfamiliar to me, yet their sentiment was plain enough: it was a song of pilgrimage and suffering, and long-delayed reward.

Gentlemen, it shall not in the least surprise you to learn that my wife and I had not been in the custom of sharing a bed since the earliest days of our marriage. At the time that these events took place, Alice and I had become accustomed to slumbering in bedrooms at opposite ends of the great first storey.

I had dreamed not at all but when I woke, as well of those phenomena which I have already described, I become aware that the scent of the draper's widow still lingered on my skin.

I rose quickly, hung a blanket about me, for you will recall how cavernous and draughty are the rooms of that house, and hurried along the hallway, past the ranks of mahogany panelling and towards the source of the disturbance. As I walked, I understood that Fieldwick Hall itself seemed different. It was as though some process of thawing were already taking place, as if it were returning to life.

I found them in the library, the place from which she had first spied him. The singing had stopped. There was only one mouth from which it could have issued. Indeed, the stranger still stood somewhat in the posture of performance, upright in the centre of the room. My wife was seated appreciatively on a seat beside that section of the bookcase that was given over to the history of Imperial Rome.

Just as the house seemed to be undergoing some process of resuscitation so also did Alice. Her eyes were brighter. Her hands were clasped together as though in scarcely-suppressed excitement and her lips were turned upwards in an expression of delight. As I saw her then in that tableau she seemed at least a decade younger than her true age and I remembered, dimly, as though a familiar voice were calling my name from faraway, just what it was that first had drawn me to the lady.

When others have asked me since – as you gentlemen will no doubt ask in due course – why it was that I permitted the stranger to stay for so long, know that in large part the answer was this: he made my wife more happy than I had ever managed to achieve.

You may say – and you may very well be right to say – that this great mistake of mine was born in large part from that quantity of guilt and shame which I carted about with me in those days and which, naive though it sounds to me now, I could not then conceive of enlarging.

I shall say nothing further in my defence except that motive is a complicated thing, understood least of all by he who is driven by it.

At my entrance, both Alice and the stranger turned to face me. I saw that they had eaten a peasant's breakfast of bread and cheese. The interloper smiled, hastened towards me, his hands outstretched and said: "You must be Mr Greene?" Then, warmly: "Nathaniel?"

I said that I was.

"Then, sir, I owe you a great debt of gratitude. Indeed, together with your remarkable wife, I do believe I owe you both my life."

I inclined my head in such a way as to suggest I knew very well that he spoke the truth. "Who are you, sir?" I asked. "How came you to this place?"

He smiled up at me – a rather bony sight given how closely hung to his skull was the lean flesh of his face – though I saw nonetheless an echo in it nonetheless of something which would once have been charm. "Now those, my dear Mr Greene, are questions which are not easily answered."

My own expression hardened. "I should have thought them simple enough."

The newcomer cast his eyes down towards the ground. "Still they are, I fear... not as very simple as all that."

My wife was by my side now, though I had not noticed her steal there. "We know that he is Victor," she said softly. "For the present that must be enough."

I began to marshal my objections, but Alice placed a hand upon my left arm and squeezed it once.

"Please," she said. "His memory... He has been through some great upheaval. He remembers only stray glimpses and moments."

I looked at the fellow and he would not look back.

"The authorities—" I began but this time I was interrupted by Victor's hands on mine.

"Please." There was a strange symmetry with his petitioning

and that of my wife. "Just give me a little time here. Safe and secure. I will not stay for long. Just for a day or so. Then you will be rid of me. And I can give you – give both of you – something in return."

"Oh? And what might that be?"

He met my gaze and I saw in his eyes weird knowledge burning there.

"Why," he said, in the manner of an imp from a fireside tale. "I can give you your heart's desire."

- 8 -
A PROPOSAL

I withdrew not long after this remark and I spent the remainder of the morning in a condition of uncertainty. I took myself to my study and kept to myself in there, still most unclear as to how any of this had come to pass, how I had been rendered so uneasy in my own home while a stranger seemed to have the run of the place. I tried to concentrate upon my book, upon my survey of London folklore, yet I found that I was wholly unable to do so.

From a distance, I heard the voices of my wife and the interloper raised in animated conversation. The sounds too of sincere laughter. I paced about my room and once or twice I stepped out into the corridor, half-hoping, I suppose, to catch the substance of their discourse, only to be able to make out nothing more than confidential-sounding murmurings.

Shortly before noon, I saw them, the pair of them, from my window taking a turn together still deep in secret discussion, her arm looped firmly around his. For a man who had, only the night before, collapsed from frailty and exhaustion, he appeared to be moving with considerable speed and strength.

For years my wife had spurned all warmth or kindness of any kind, yet here she was, close and friendly, with a man who appeared to me to be nothing more than a stray, albeit a well-mannered one. I watched them and wondered, and tried not to think of that odd resonance between what the draper's widow had said to me (her father's warning) and that which had already begun to unfold before my eyes.

I turned aside and went to fetch myself a meal (Mr and Mrs Tebb still being absent) and walked through that empty house without ever once being able to shake the impossible conviction that I was in some fashion being observed.

Under the lackadaisical supervision of Mrs Tebb, the kitchen had become a dark and malodorous place. I did not linger there, but fetched bread and cold meat from the pantry and prepared a rough luncheon. I ate it swiftly and without pleasure, standing upright, listening for the sounds of people above me, in the manner of a lazy domestic.

This done, I stole back towards my sanctuary only to see my wife approach along the corridor. At first, she did not speak at the sight of me but only put a finger against her lips.

"Hush, Nathaniel. Our friend is sleeping now."

"Is he a friend?" I asked and the acerbity of my tone was no accident. "It seems to me that we know nothing at all about him."

She sighed, as though I was an absurdly unreasonable creature. "I have spoken with him for many hours. He is a most remarkable man."

I scoffed. "He might be anyone! A mountebank, a beggar, a madman, a thief..."

"He is none of those things."

"How do you know that?"

"He has told me much of his life. I have heard how he has suffered and something of what he might have achieved... had others not sought to thwart him at every turn."

"Has he no family? No friends? No-one who is searching for him? He surely cannot stay here."

My wife smiled. "But he wants to stay now. He says he likes it here. He says that he believes that this might be the perfect place for him to continue his work... What he calls his experiments..."

"What kind of work? What sort of experiments?"

"He says he is a natural philosopher."

I snorted. "Such a description might cover a multitude of sins."

She stepped near towards me; twice now in a handful of hours we had been closer than we had for years.

"Nathaniel, please. He has made me a proposal."

"A what?"

"He says that he can give us what we have always longed for."

I could not at that moment imagine what she might possibly mean. "And what is that? Enough hints."

When she spoke again there was a fervour in her eyes such as I had never seen before. "He says he can give us a child."

- 9 -

THE JUDGE'S HOUSE

Out again I went after this, her mad words still echoing in my mind. Back I went on horseback in the low, oppressive light of a winter's afternoon, back in flight but not towards the coast and my fair widow, but instead towards the nearest town, a place which you gentlemen have not, I believe, yet had the pleasure of visiting: a town named Nevisham Row. It is the smallest of towns, barely more than a village, though it did boast one remarkable and influential inhabitant.

The animal beneath me appeared to sense the urgency of our mission and seemed swifter than before. I remember the drumming of hoofbeats on the country lanes as we surged towards our destination. I remember thinking of the warning of the dead man.

I was there in less than half an hour, first hammering on the door of that singular individual who was known to all in the district as "the Judge", then being ushered in by his maidservant, Cassie, then being seated in his little parlour before a blazing fire, then greeting the man himself with handshakes of the heartiest kind, then telling him all that had occurred, at least to the degree that one gentleman ever tells another the entire details of his own life. When I had finished the story, ending at the point at which Alice had spoken that blasphemous proposal by our visitor, the Judge leaned forward and held me in his decisive gaze. The room was hot and he, a large, rubicund man, two decades my senior, dressed as if for an altogether draughtier house, was perspiring to a notable degree.

"That's damn strange," he said. "A damn strange thing!"

"You can see why I came to you?"

"Of course, of course... Whoever this fellow is and wherever he has sprung from there will be something criminal at the heart of it, I have no doubt."

"I need him removed, Judge," I said. "But it must be done legally and without any unnecessary distress caused to my wife.

In many respects, we each have proved a disappointment to the other but I would have her feel any... superfluous pain."

He nodded. "You are a good man, Nathaniel. A good man!"

I frowned. "I do not believe that to be true. But I would not have her be let down by this foreigner. He is an obvious charlatan and a fraud."

The judge gave a single, curt nod which indicated that his mind was made up. Such a brisk nod had once, before his retirement, sentenced fifteen men and four women to the gallows. "You may leave the matter in my hands, Nathaniel. No, no, do not reach for your pocketbook, I shall not hear of it. I owe you a good deal, after all, for what you did once for me in Hunstanton."

I smiled, remembering. "It was nothing. No more than any man might have some for his friend."

"Well, then."

He rose to his feet and extended his hand. "Thank you for your visitation. It is indeed a thing to be regretted that you should have had this viper slither into your midst. I will need a day to make the necessary preparations. Can you stand to have the fellow with you for another night?"

"Naturally," I said. "Though of course I shall sleep with one eye open." Then I said something very foolish which I long have regretted. "The man may be a liar yet I do not believe that he, at least in the strictest physical terms, poses any immediate threat. He is harmless enough, I dare say, and can be left to fester."

We shook hands. "Godspeed," said the Judge.

"And to you," said I.

I turned and I was at the doorway when he asked the question.

"Do you still see the draper's widow?"

I did not look back to face him. "On occasion."

The older man chuckled softly. The crackle and hiss of the fire. "She always was a lovely girl."

Without meaning to have done so, I had bunched my left hand into a fist. I felt the press of my nails into my palm. Carefully, I uncurled my fingers. "She has her points."

"I am just too old for it now." The judge spoke on though I did not wish to hear his words. "Embers, sir. Smouldering embers. That is all that is left now for me."

As if in sardonic rebuke to this metaphor the fire spat behind us.

"Still," he said. "Do give her my warmest regards. Should you happen to meet with her again."

"Yes, Judge," I murmured. "I shall most certainly do so."

Without saying more, I stepped out of the room, down the hallway and out of the house, leaving a place of warmth again and going back into the cold.

- 10 -
A TROUBLING EXCHANGE OF WORDS

It was almost dark by the time that I came home and the heat of the Judge's hearth had long since left me. The horse, unaccustomed to such frequent excursions, whinnied in pitiful complaint as I returned her to the stables. I cursed once again as I did so the continuing absence of our last remaining servants.

The Hall, as before, seemed oddly unfamiliar to me as I walked its corridors, less empty and more urgent than it had been in a long time. There were now no voices raised and, mercifully, no singing either, yet were there lamps burning and candles lit in rooms which had not seen any illumination besides daylight for many months.

I went on, feeling more than ever like a stranger in that which ought by rights to have been mine. I did not call out, either my wife's name or that of the newcomer. I sought solace in the library and, as I walked, I did my best to assure myself that we had only hours left of this unhappy intrusion and that, thanks to the Judge, matters would be set right upon the morrow. For some reason, the notion did little to comfort me.

The cuckoo was in the library, of course, sitting alone with several volumes laid out before him, as though he were a prince and this his counting-house. Still, he possessed the good grace to look startled at my entrance.

He got hurriedly to his feet, with greater alacrity than should have been possible given his earlier, supposed condition, and looked at me with a quality of surprise that seemed a little too theatrical to be altogether unfeigned.

"Which of my books are you reading, sir?" I asked. "And may I enquire as to the present whereabouts of my wife?"

The fellow looked discomfited at the cadence of my words.

"I am reading a book of scripture," he said and indeed he was, though I noted at a glance that the volume was one of certain apocryphal chronicles which had for many centuries faced a determined programme of suppression. "And I thank you most sincerely for the loan of it. As to your dear wife, Alice, she is sleeping upstairs. From all that she has told me her life is generally one that is barren of incident. My own interruption into it I fear has caused her some distress." He affected a mournful demeanour. "But, please, Mr Greene, I must thank you again, from the bottom of my heart, for your great kindness and hospitality."

He went on in this vein a good while longer though I could not tell you gentlemen one more word of what he said. A kind of shroud settled over me and I heard a great rushing in my ears, as of the seething tide.

How dare this gargoyle squat in my own library? How dare his shadow hang so heavy in my house in but a day of his unasked for arrival? I reached out and seized the scrawny wrist of his left hand. His skin was cold and dry.

"Who are you?" I cried. "Who are you truly?"

He had by now ceased his prattling. There was an awful silence between us. I tightened my grip around his wrist.

"How did you come here? What do you want with us? What lies have you been whispering to Alice?"

At the last of my questions a look of indescribable cunning passed over his face and I felt that I was seeing for the first time something of the real man.

"I have told her no lies," he said softly. "I have promised her nothing which is impossible."

"She said... she said you had promised her a child."

"And that is what she wants, is it not? More than anything else? And that is what you have so evidently failed to give her?"

I do believe that he imagined this last barb would enrage me to some act of force for, as he spoke the words, I could feel his arm tense beneath me as if in anticipation of a blow. Instead, I released him and stood back.

"The fault is not mine, sir. It is hers."

The visitor rubbed at his wrist, at the place where I had

held him. "Nonetheless, I can give her what she wants."

"How?" I all but spat the word.

That look of profound cunning returned to his features. "The method is of no conventional sort." His gaze settled on a point above us, as though something invisible hung above me. "It has been tried before though it shall be successful this time."

"What do you mean, you goblin?"

He stepped closer to me, seemingly unafraid. "I can bring new life to the world," he said. "I can stitch together the old to create an original thing. I have done it before. I can do it again."

Closer, he came. Curiously, I let him do so. I did not stop him nor did I stumble back.

I saw it then, something of what my wife had seen in him from the first — his strange, persuasive power.

"Look at me," he said, and I did as he had asked. "See my eyes. You know that I am in earnest. You know that I speak the truth. You know that I can do what I have pledged to do."

There was another awful silence then and I did indeed see in his dark eyes sincerity and passion and something which might have been either genius or insanity.

At last, I stepped away. I turned my back upon him and I walked at some speed from my own library. He called nothing after me and I heard no sound of movement. It was almost as I imagine a haunting must be — as though he were merely a spectre and that, had I gone back that chamber, I would have found it empty and the visitor vanished into air.

In my own room, I closed the door and sat heavily upon my bed, my mind in uproar. It felt as if I had taken strong drink or some other, stranger substance. It was then that I noticed a note upon my pillow. I recognised at once the handwriting of my wife. It was composed of but four words, the lettering forceful and determined.

It ran as follows, and I felt at the sight of it, ice slither through my veins:

He will need <u>materials</u>.

- 11 -
IN THE NIGHTTIME

No time is more disquieting at which to wake than the hour of about three in the morning.

Nothing good should be walking abroad then, when all innocent things are abed. If ever I wake at such a point, long after midnight, and yet, a great while before the dawn, I close my eyes, turn over and force myself back into slumber.

Yet such a thing was not possible on the night after the confrontation in the library. I had flung my wife's note upon the floor and fallen, still half-dressed, into a fretful doze.

I was woken with quiet urgency by a hand upon my shoulder and by a familiar voice: "Sir, wake up, sir! Quickly now!"

At the sound of it, I startled awake, sat upright and looked about me, wild and disordered. Before I could speak, the person in the room spoke gruffly: "Hush now, sir. Keep your voice low."

I looked and saw my manservant, Mr Tebb, standing beside my bed, his stocky figure shadowed in the moonlight.

He was a little man, Tebb, short and once well built,

though running badly now to fat and with a pinched red face which spoke of his fondness for the bottle.

"Tebb?" I hissed. "What is the meaning of this unwarranted intrusion?"

He crouched down a little nearer to me. You will no doubt consider, gentlemen, that such unusual familiarity is sadly indicative of the degree to which I had permitted arrangements between us to descend and I should not care this afternoon to disagree.

The words of Mr Tebb were urgent and low. "There is a stranger in this house, sir. And the fellah is shameless! Sleeping in a bed as easy as you like. Snug, sir. That's how he looks. Snug as a new-born baby in a drawer."

He drew in a breath through his bulbous nose, evidently pleased with himself for the vigour of his imagery.

"You want me to throw him out then, sir? You want me to make an example of him?"

The relish in his voice, I fear, did Mr Tebb little credit. "I'll move him quickly, sir, and take him into the grounds. It wouldn't disturb your lady at all."

For an instant, I was tempted. Tebb was no strongman but he was well-proportioned and certainly large enough to overpower our slender, uninvited guest.

Perhaps, I thought, I need not have turned to the Judge at all? Perhaps Mr Tebb – faithful, if morbidly thirsty Mr Tebb – who had stayed by my side when so many others had abandoned me... Perhaps he was the man to free me of this interloper?

"The gentleman..." I began, haltingly, "is a friend of my wife's... Though not altogether, I confess, a welcome one."

"I thought so, sir, yes. I could sense it, sir, I could smell it on him. A wrong 'un, that one, from skin to core." The eagerness was rising. "Let me throw him out, sir. Let me rid you of that canker."

I saw then how it might go – the visitor taken swiftly from his room, Tebb's big right hand clamped to the man's mouth to silence his protestations, a swift, brutal struggle in the woods outside, then a fresh beggar loosed upon the countryside, bruised and even a little wounded but moving with weary determination, away from us, away from the Hall, away from Crispin Rye, heading south again, perhaps, drifting towards London where he would be swallowed up by the teeming masses, and disappear, never to be heard of. The thought was pleasing to me in its elegant simplicity. Alice would be furious, naturally – but when was she not?

The unpleasantness would pass in time and we would return to our previous state of dormancy. It was a stage through which I was quite happy to pass if only I could be rid of the intruder.

"Tebb?" I said and I think that, at my tone, he divined something of my purpose.

"Yes, sir?"

I was about to tell him to do what he must in order to evict our wretched new tenant only to hear a hurried pacing outside the door and then the turning of the handle.

At such an hour and in such a room, one still filled with shadow, we both fairly jumped at the noise. A number of terrible possibilities presented themselves to me only for them to be, at least in part, dispelled by the sight of my wife on the threshold to my chamber, dressed in her nightgown and, holding out before her, in the manner of a figure from some melodrama of the stage, a flaming candelabra.

She did not even so much as glance at me but gave her sole attention to Mr Tebb.

"Leave him," she said and in her voice authority was to be found to a greater degree that I had heard there in a long time.

"My dear—" I began, but with a simple gesture of her hand, she silenced me.

"Tebb, you will leave that man be. You will bring him whatever he needs. You will not question me nor will you question our guest at any time or for any reason. Do you understand me?"

She raised her voice on these last two words for the servant had turned his head to look at me, no doubt for guidance and advice.

"Do not look at him," said my wife. "Never look at him. Not any longer."

Tebb disobeyed this command and received an immediate rebuke for it.

"Mr Tebb!"

He looked into her eyes and saw there, I fancy, indications of her iron will. A long moment paused. He nodded.

"Yes, ma'am."

Mr Tebb left the room without looking back. In this fashion, was my last potential ally in the house taken from me.

Alice looked glacially towards me. "You saw my message?"

I said that I had.

"Good. He shall prepare for you a list."

"Alice—" I began. Yet she too had already gone and closed the door behind her with a deliberation which suggested that she believed herself to be in sole command.

I simply wriggled down into my bed and willed the night

to be over. Yet she does not know about the Judge, I thought to myself, as I returned to an uneasy sleep. The Judge will come tomorrow and he will bring help and this strange interruption will be brought to its overdue conclusion.

It seems absurd that I even permitted myself to believe for a moment in this disastrous fallacy.

- 12 -

CERTAIN PREPARATIONS ARE BEGUN

I dreamed for what was left of that night of the draper's widow and of the words that her late father had delivered. The dream itself was a stark and minatory thing: no corner of my life, it seemed, could now be entirely free.

The world that greeted me when I awoke was changed only in subtle ways from that of the preceding day, the process being, in some sense, very gradual, as of an apple, left out for too long on a summer's afternoon, submitting to the processes of decay. There was a sourness to the house again now that the Tebbs had returned, combined, I supposed, with a sense of some unseen mechanism devoted to the escalation of events.

Upon waking, I rang my bell and Mr Tebb appeared almost at once, a breakfast tray held out tremblingly before him.

"Mr Tebb..." I began, but he put the items down with a harsh clatter upon my cabinet and turned away and went towards the door.

"Tebb!" I said shortly, and he stopped.

Yet still he would not face me.

"What is our guest doing today?" I asked. "How does he conduct himself?"

Tebb's voice was low and maddeningly inconsequential.

"Mr Victor's in the East Wing, sir. He says he has to make certain… preparations."

"Is he now? And does he indeed?"

Still the man did not turn to me.

"Tell me, Mr Tebb, are you not in the least curious as to what these preparations might entail? And as to precisely what it is for which he is preparing?"

The voice of Mr Tebb was very soft and very quiet then, as of a misbehaving child confessing to his tutor.

"I am not privy, sir, to the particulars of the thing. No, no. But Mrs Greene has spoken to me again, sir, and to Mrs Tebb also and I am given to understand that our guest is some sort of miracle worker, sir, even mayhaps some species of… angel."

"Indeed? Is that what you have been told?"

"Yes, sir, it is, sir."

I was about to inform the servant that I did not believe our visitor to be any such thing, that it was my considered opinion that he was nothing but a trickster of the worst kind, his only special gift a rare facility for persuasion – also that his mere presence caused me grave concern and that I would do a great deal indeed to secure his immediate eviction. Yet, before I could speak, Tebb scurried from the room and closed the door behind me, a mouse hastening from some approaching broom.

I did not call after him but only sighed and, with determination, set about my breakfast.

Having eaten, completed my toilet and dressed, I went in search of our rogue lodger, seeking not, upon this occasion, confirmation but merely a little necessary understanding.

I did not have to search the house but only to follow the sounds of hammering and work which led me, as Tebb had suggested, to the East Wing.

Now, gentlemen, I am not certain if you will be able to recall it but there is in that quarter of the building a large, high-ceilinged room with was once used in elder days for dancing and for hospitality, though we had never pressed it into service to that end.

Instead, it had been left quite empty and had been closed up, filled by then with nothing but echoes and dust. Now all was different. The stranger was present. On that morning, he was an exemplar of energy, giving orders to Mr Tebb while my wife looked on, her every aspect indicative of the handmaiden to the high priest.

He was constructing something, with space for much more to come.

"Mr Tebb, hurry! The pulley, my friend! Raise it as high as you are able. Fetch more timber! And I will have need also of an empty bathtub…"

I watched from the doorway, unobserved by all.

Victor's instructions were innocuous to the point of banality – to the point, in fact, of inadvertent comedy – yet I divined something sinister all the same in the cadence of his demands. I shook my head and retired, meaning to take myself off to the foxhole of my study and there await the arrival of the Judge.

On my way I passed the female servant of the house, the first time I had seen her in three days. She said nothing but only looked up at me with a sly smile on her face, suggestive of some novel boldness for which I did not care at all.

I hurried past and went to my room. I cannot say entirely why but, as I sat in there and waited, I was sure to lock the door, an act which gave me some degree of obscure contentment.

- 13 -
A THWARTING

I did my best to concentrate as I waited and to continue to work on my great almanac of London lore and legend, a labour of considerable thoroughness and ambition which sadly now will never be completed – unless hands which are not my own one day bring it to a finish.

You need not eye me so, gentlemen, for I should not dream of asking strangers to so much as consider such a task. Still, on that day the words would not come to me and I dare say that the lights of civilisation which once had been the stuff of my daily life had rarely seemed so far away. I felt, perhaps, an inkling of what my wife had felt for years – that existence here was a state of isolation, as though we resided on some small lozenge of land cut off from the mainland by a high tide.

She had said to me once, some years before, at the end of a long, sultry summer's day in which we had done nothing but drowse: "I shall go mad here, Nathaniel, I know that I shall, unless we people this house with others. Even one, just one, would be sufficient to stave it away…" I shivered a little at the recollection and wondered anew at certain of my actions.

Curiously, given what was about to unfold, my gaze drifted

about my room, alighting on a book of local history, a dry affair written by a deceased apothecary. I picked it up and even went so far as to leaf through its pages in a desultory fashion. Sentences and paragraphs swam before me as though I were in a state of high fever. I set the thing aside and waited.

In this fashion the morning passed. Lunch came after — another tray delivered by Mr Tebb and left outside my still-locked door.

The early hours of the afternoon went by still more slowly and the first, crepuscular shadows of the evening had begun to appear before I finally heard the sounds for which I had been waiting — that of men on horseback approaching Fieldwick Hall and, together with the agreeable noise of male conversation, the firm, stern voice of my friend chief amongst the palaver.

With unmatched relief, I rose, unlocked my door and hastened downwards to greet he whom I believed to be my saviour.

The Judge was, in those first moments when I flung open the door to him, in a state of great and confident expectation. His broad face was flushed red, and he was flanked by three other fellows, all of them strangers to me but of a type that was at once recognisable, with the look of men who are willing, at the slightest invitation, to conduct acts of violence. That the Judge could raise up such a triumvirate at the slightest notice did not surprise me in the least.

"Nathaniel!" There was a swagger to him that afternoon as the winter darkness began to fall. "Is he here still? The scoundrel, is he within?"

"He is," I said. "He is... working."

"Very well. I mean to have a word with him. The names of

these gentlemen you do not need to know for now for I hope we shall have no need of them."

I glanced again at his companions.

"Infantry?" I said.

The Judge only nodded and shouldered on past me into the lounge, his hired ruffians at his heels.

For the second time in that week, but on this occasion more unexpectedly, I felt myself the subject of a discomfiting intrusion.

Past me they went, the Judge and his familiars, into the main body of the house.

I heard my friend call out. "Frankenstein! Frankenstein, where are you, man?"

I closed the door, thrust aside any ill feeling and hastened after the arrivals. They were, I appreciated, making a deliberate show of it, with their thunderous boots and their loud voices and their general manner of huntsmen in pursuit of the stag.

Having seen for myself the strange imperturbability of our visitor, I had my doubts as to the wisdom of the stratagem yet I followed them all the same, up to the open door of the old ballroom outside of which the Judge and his three friends had stopped.

My wife emerged, seeming quite unruffled by the interruption.

"Good afternoon, gentlemen! I fear that my husband neglected to tell me of your intention to call upon us." At this, she gave me a quick, savage glance. "Have you come to see our guest?"

The Judge, who had, perhaps, been expecting some series of protestations and entreaties seemed surprised by her demeanour. "We have, madam, yes," he said, and I heard in his voice that his stride up the staircase and along the hallways had caused him to become short of breath. He was also perspiring in spite of the cold.

My wife smiled at him and at his retinue of gargoyles. "Well, you had better come in and meet Victor. We have, after all, been expecting you. Or, if not you precisely, then at least someone very like you."

The Judge seemed to hesitate. He looked back at me, then at his associates. Then I heard a voice rising out from within the chamber: the cool, calm voice of the visitor.

"Please, sir, do step inside. I expect there are matters you wish to discuss."

At this piece of effrontery, the Judge found his fire.

He bellowed: "You can be assured of that, sir!"

Then, like a lion tamer meaning to enter the ring, he turned to me, to Alice and to the soldiers. "Wait here. All of you. I've little doubt that I can resolve the issue. Should anything further be needed, I shall call for you."

He held up one hand to ward off my wife who had, I thought, opened her mouth in preparation of some objection or other.

"No, madam, I must do this alone. Man to man."

She smiled with unusual sweetness. "I understand. But I meant merely to offer you and your companions refreshment should you so wish."

The Judge looked suspicious at this invitation, as well he might. "Thank you, madam, but no."

He looked me in the eye, nodded once and stepped inside, closing the door adroitly behind him. My wife still acted as though this were a dinner party of her own devising. "Shall we retire downstairs?" she asked. "While the two gentlemen conduct their business?"

She looked at our faces, set and determined. "No? Very well, I shall leave you here. Nathaniel, I must speak to Mr Tebb about some... new materials. You will find me with the servants if you wish to speak with me once we are alone again."

She smiled again at the three men and walked away down the hallway. One of the soldiers — burly and ruddy-faced — said, without looking at me: "Something's wrong."

"How so?" I asked, although I knew he spoke the truth.

"With all of it," he said, and his words hung there in the silence between us as we waited.

From the other side, we heard only murmurings, two low voices, both courteous at first, that of the Judge, a firm determined thing and those of the guest softer but no less forceful in its way. Of specific words or phrases we heard nothing at all.

Certain looks were exchanged amongst we four patient gentlemen but nothing further was said between us. From beyond, the drone of discussion went on for a surprising duration for I had hoped that the matter would prove in the end to be a simple one, to be resolved by the Judge by way of a few sharp sentences and, at worst, a single, implicit threat. Evidently, the issue was not to be dealt with so simply.

In the event, the interruption to this long and awkward demi-silence came from my own side of the door.

The youngest of the three men, the one whose voice I had yet to hear, said suddenly: "Mr Greene?"

"Yes?"

The fellow looked about him with a degree of uncertainty which had not been suggested by his earlier swagger. "This house of yours, sir... Fieldwick Hall..." He was evidently a local man and his words were flecked with the accent of the region.

"Yes?" I said.

"I have been here before, sir."

"Indeed?"

"Yes, sir. As a child, sir. It had – forgive me – but it had an evil reputation then. I never thought I would ever set foot in here again." And he looked about him once more.

"Why?" I asked.

"Saw something, sir, didn't I?"

"What did you see here?" I asked him. "Or, rather, what did you believe that you saw?"

He looked a little ashen at my question. He hesitated yet I think he was about to answer me when we all heard a most terrific cry emanating from the adjacent room, mere yards from where we stood.

It was a cry of startled outrage, yes, but it also betokened something more, for it possessed a quality of what sounded unmistakably like fear.

You will have guessed, gentlemen, that this noise came not from our European visitor but from the Judge himself. It was a sound of which I would not before that afternoon have believed him to have been capable. The men looked about them in concern and with surprise.

One called out. "Sir, what is the matter?"

Another strode to the door and pulled it rudely open. The third man, he who had been speaking to me a moment before, touched me lightly on the arm and spoke swiftly. "You asked me, sir, and since you asked me I will answer. It was a child, sir. It was the spectre of a crooked child."

Then, before he could say more, the figure of the Judge himself came bustling through the now open door, his face a picture of most uncharacteristic agitation.

"I have to go," he said and he would not look at me in the eye. "I have to leave at once."

He motioned to his men. "With me, with me!"

"Sir?"

He waved away this footling objection. "We have to leave this house, gentlemen! Immediately!"

I caught at his arm. "What is it? What happened in there?"

He brushed my hand away. "Not now."

He looked at me, though only briefly. "I will write to you," he said. "I will explain. For now – it must suffice to say that I am sorry."

Without further explanation, he went from me and the others with him, their heavy-footed tread sounding a retreat through all the house.

The soldier who had spoken to me was the last to leave. He gave me a quick, imploring look. "Go, sir!" was all he said before he too vanished from me.

Stunned, I listened to them in their flight. Then, from the room beyond, came a small, dry cough and the voice of the man who had won my wife's allegiance.

"Mr Greene? I am so very sorry that your friends had to leave us so suddenly."

I strode into that room then, into my room, my outrage suddenly aflame to confront the blackguard, that dreadful lizard in my midst. "What do you mean by your actions, sir?"

The blood was thundering through me. I heard its drumbeat pounding in my ears.

"What did you say to the Judge? What did you tell him? What power could you possibly wield over him?"

That little potentate sat neatly upon his throne and with a small smile of victory on his face. "I merely told him certain truths. Certain... disagreeable truths that I have learned in some of my travels to the great frontiers of human understanding."

His composure agitated me still further and I found myself quite unable to frame my objections. I discovered myself instead emitting a single, sustained snarl. I all but threw myself in the direction of Victor Frankenstein.

"Stop!" My wife's voice, high and compelling, came from the doorway. Realising that my arm was raised to strike, I lowered it, paced backwards and tried to slow my breathing. Our guest merely observed me coolly, as imperturbable as a priest hearing confession.

"Please," he said. "Please, Mr Greene. You must calm yourself."

As you will surely know, gentlemen, unless your own lives have been sheltered things indeed, there sometimes comes a moment at which one can either attempt to regain one's dignity or to surrender to urgency and distress and throw away all pretence of self-management. Upon that long ago afternoon, I chose the second course. I ran from the room, down the hallway and towards the outside, shouting all the while: "Judge! Judge! Wait!"

If either Alice or Victor Frankenstein called after me, I did not hear their voices raised. Beyond the house, three of the horsemen were already all but lost to the horizon. Only one seemed to hesitate. The Judge, upon his steed, had paused, some feet away, to gaze back at the house, his slumped, defeated posture that of the general who, in the wake of some rout of rare devastation, looks mournfully for a final time at the battlefield. In frantic motions, I waved my arms.

"Judge!" I ran towards him, my breath coming in thick, fierce pants, my flesh quivering as I went. As I have said, gentlemen, at this time all dignity had fled from me. The Judge watched my approach.

His horse seemed skittish yet he was firm with the beast and urged her to stay in her appointed place.

"What is it, Nathaniel?" he asked as soon as I was in earshot, and his tone was changed utterly from that of mere minutes before. It was flat and without nuance, like a person under the influence of some numbing medicament. "What do you want to ask me? I warn you that you will not enjoy the answers. Besides, I said – did I not? – that I would write it all in a letter?"

"What did he say? Why are you fleeing?"

The Judge looked at me with something much like pity in his eyes. "Did I not say to you once some years ago, when first you and Alice came here that you should find some other property in which to live? If memory serves, I even went so far as to make suggestions."

"I recall," I said.

"This is a place," the Judge went on, "which brings to its bosom men who have malice in their hearts."

"Superstitious nonsense," I said. "And I told you so at the time. Besides, I've seen or heard nothing whatever since to change my view."

A thin smile appeared upon the Judge's sluggish face as if etched there very slowly by some invisible hand. "Then you shall," he said. "Very soon now, you shall."

He would say no more but only turned around his mare and set his back against me and rode away, hard after his companions who had not long before exhibited such apparent fearlessness.

Tired from my exertions and labours, washed over by disappointment and by the first flickerings of despair, I watched the party go, back into the low, lean, ominous greys and browns of the Norfolk countryside. Then, squaring my shoulders, I walked back towards the house and to all that awaited me there. It felt very much as though, by doing so, I was succumbing to something approximate to destiny.

- 14 -
A FALLING AWAY

Returning to the house on that darkling afternoon, I felt rather as might a spirit in the first few hours of its earthly demise. It seemed as though I were invisible in my own dwelling-place. The Tebbs passed me in the corridors with absolute boldness and indifference. I walked into the old ballroom and saw that Victor Frankenstein and my wife were once again engaged in the construction of whichever mad contraption it was that our visitor had ordered. The man looked up when I came into the room, as coolly impassive as though he were the owner of some agreeable hostelry and I some insouciant patron.

"Was there anything further, Mr Greene?" he asked.

"Dear me, but you do look rather distressed." Alice looked over at me, smiling with a gentleness which the unobservant might have believed to be unfeigned. "You seem tired, Nathaniel. You should lie down. Take a rest. If we need you…"

At this, she exchanged with the interloper a glance of dreadful conspiracy. "Why, we will be sure to let you know."

You will think me weak, gentlemen, but there was something in the awful sincerity of their gaze that made me do as they asked and retreat once again, wounded and bewildered, back to the eyrie of my study. I had a bottle secreted in there – no, two bottles; no, three – and I fear I took solace in them for the rest of that long evening. It had been a while indeed since last I had sunk with gratitude into the pleasure of the grape and I had no longer the stomach or the stamina for it. I drank alone and I was not disturbed. By midnight, I had slipped into a kind of a vague, merciful forgetting.

There were sounds in the house that night, sounds of hammering and of construction as well as other, stranger noises – of comings and goings, of hushed voices. Once, I heard footsteps. Once, I heard what seemed to be the high-pitched wail of a cat. Yet I took myself to bed, a glass for accompaniment and I went to sleep and I did my best to hope that all would be different in the morning.

Gentlemen, the long days that followed represented for me and for all that had ever been good or just in that house, a kind of inexorable falling away. I am not proud of my behaviour during this span of time. I kept to my rooms and I kept to the bottle.

You look at me with disappointment, gentlemen. You think me a coward or a milksop? It was not so. Rather, it was as though our guest had brought with him a kind of enchantment and we all, my wife, the servants and I, languished under his spell. When I was not drunk or melancholic I roamed the fields and woodlands which surrounded our little village. I took myself on occasion to The Mariner's Rest where I was greeted with suspicion or else ignored entirely and left to stew in silent isolation.

I have said that this lasted for days yet it felt more like months. I wonder now how he – how Victor Frankenstein – achieved so much in so short a span of time. He had been planning for this opportunity for a long while, I think. He no longer had the luxury of apprenticeship. He knew he must be swift.

And so the work went on around me. The transformation of the ballroom, the weird sounds in the night, the scurrying intensity of Mr and Mrs Tebb as they went about their new business on the orders of their new master. My wife treated me rather as she might have done a distant family member who had come to stay following the irreversible decline of their faculties, which I suppose was not so very far from the truth.

Were they drugging me? Was there something in the wine? Or in the food which was brought to me by the Tebbs – now shuffling and reproachful in their manner – three times a day?

Perhaps there was. All I can say for certain is that for a period of five weeks, I was not myself at all. I stumbled and I dreamed.

Then, one morning – the eighth of March – I woke feeling a little more clear-headed than had by then become normal. You may be interested, gentlemen, to learn, that I had barely touched my supper of the night before. So I took myself away, out of my home and off to the house of the Judge in Nevisham Row, only to find that residence locked and bolted with no sign whatever of recent habitation.

I poked around in the weeds that were growing up against the walls and I peered in at the dark and dingy windows. The air was crisp and the sky was grey; it was a scene which spoke of sad abandonment.

"Can I help you?" The voice was cracked and aged. I turned to see a little old man, bent with decrepitude, looking up at me from under thick, dark brows.

"I was looking for the Judge."

"Gone," the old man said in a shrill, peremptory tone. "Five weeks past. Gone in the night like a guilty man. Or like a debtor."

He snorted and pushed his stick into the cold ground.

"And he left nothing behind?" I asked. "No address? No means of finding him?"

The old man shook his head. "Not so far as I know."

"He was…" I began, falteringly. "He was to write me a letter. A letter of explanation."

The old man looked at me levelly, an element of appraisal to his gaze. "You Greene?" he asked.

"I am," I said, "I am Nathaniel Greene."

The old man scrutinised me as though he suspected me of some mendacity. "History man, are you? Collector of fairy tales?"

I inclined my head in acknowledgement. He shot me one final glance of doubt.

"Then perhaps he did leave something… on secondary thoughts, sir, yes, perhaps he did leave something. Just for you."

"Oh? And what was that then?"

He looked at me and said nothing at all. I reached into my pocket and handed him a coin. He nodded his thanks, showing, for the first time, the merest hint of deference.

"Two things," he said. "Two things the Judge told me as to tell you. The first – simple enough – leave that house."

"And my wife?" I asked bitterly. "Am I to leave her too? Am I to leave that man my every possession?"

The old gentleman seemed to have not the least interest in my questions.

"I can tell you only what I was told, sir. That's all. Just a messenger is what I am."

I sighed. "And the second thing?"

"You have a visitor at your home? Yes? A man who spoke with the Judge alone?"

"That is so."

"Well, the Judge's words on that particular matter aren't particularly clear to me, sir. That is – they don't make a deal of sense and I dare say they weren't supposed to."

"What was it?" I grew impatient. "What did the Judge instruct you to say?"

He looked reluctant and for a moment I thought that I would have no choice but to reach again for my small store of currency.

Then he spoke six words which have stayed with me long after their speaking, even now, even after I know so much more of monsters and of reanimation.

What the little old man said to me on that clear March morning was this: "Frankenstein speaks daily with the dead."

He met my gaze then and would not look away.

"Was there no more?" I asked.

"That's all I know, sir. So will you listen to him? Will you take the Judge's advice and leave?"

"No," I said, affronted by the man's tone of unearned familiarity. "I cannot and I will not go. I feel sure that I must stay and…"

"Yes, sir?"

"Bear witness," I said feebly and my voice did not sound quite like my own. I turned and left the little old man and began the journey home to Crispin Rye. The sky was darkening. Clouds promised rain. In the distance – the threat of some approaching thunder.

- 15 -
A DRINK OR TWO BEFORE THE STORM

You will be familiar, gentlemen, with the emotions that are engendered by the realisation that a storm is approaching. The elements are in a state of considerable agitation. The air seems almost to tremble. The shadows of the earth grow longer and darker, and there is to the world a quality of dreadful expectation. One feels as one might standing at a precipice before some inevitable drop. This was the presiding spirit of that afternoon when I left the shuttered-up house of the Judge and the cryptic injunctions of that aged man and took myself on the road back home.

That a tempest would be upon us was without question yet I believed that I might have time enough to stop out before returning to the house, for but a single drink.

Would you, gentlemen, have cared to go back to that building? With all the strange secrets that lay inside? The weird, suggestive construction in the old ballroom? The troubling understanding between my wife, the stranger and the servants? The talk, murky yet relentless, of "preparation" and "materials"?

No, sirs. Home, no longer felt like home to me and I knew I could not face it as a sober man. And so it was that I rode to that little inn which lay in the village adjacent to Crispin Rye – an inn by the name of The Deacon's Resort.

It was a gloomy, ill-favoured place with a hostile landlord, a most limited selection of food and drink and a pervasive atmosphere of sour suspicion. I had always rather liked it.

On that darkening afternoon it was still more poorly patronised than usual. Indeed, there was but one other customer in the place, making halting conversation with the bald, crumpled figure of the proprietor, Mr Ague. I saw upon my entry that the drinker was none other than the tall, angular personage of our vicar, the Reverend Leigh-Stanley, whose acquaintance I believe you gentlemen have already made.

His dark frock coat fluttered around his bony frame as he turned to greet me. In his eyes was a look of suspicion at my arrival and (unless I imagined it, which I do not believe I did) a dash of pity also.

"Nathaniel! You are an unexpected sight."

"As are you, Reverend," I said, rather enjoying his slight discomfiture.

He waved a hand as if to smooth away some imagined fleet of objections to his presence in such an institution at such an hour.

"I rose early…" he murmured, "a day of labours… a troublesome parishioner…"

He stopped speaking, saw my expression, understood how little I cared and said, simply: "Now will you permit me to get you a drink?"

It was in this fashion that I came to spend the last hours

before the culmination of the Frankenstein experiment, drinking in the company of a man of the cloth. "You know," he began, once the two of us had found a nook by the window, away from the sardonic gaze of the proprietor, "I had been meaning to pay you a visit."

I looked down and saw that I had already drained my glass. "Indeed?" I said. "For any particular reason? Or from purely social motives?"

To his considerable credit, Leigh-Stanley now looked truly unsettled. "I have heard things. Disquieting things, if there be but a scrap of truth to them. Still, my dear fellow, I can see that you are thirsty today. Let me fetch you another and then let us speak more. Perhaps there are even matters that you wish to discuss with me?"

It must have been the pressures of recent weeks stirred together with my conversation with the old man at the Judge's house and the very darkest of my suspicions but I scarcely noticed Leigh-Stanley's disappearance and reappearance, holding out a second brimming flagon. Time seemed to me at that point a little uncertain and confused.

"Nathaniel."

The vicar's hand was on my shoulder. The glass was set before me.

"Please, tell me what is happening at the Hall. Speak plainly and tell me what it is that is troubling you."

"We have a guest," I said simply. "His name is Frankenstein."

At these words, the older man looked pensive. "I've heard whispers of such a person. A gaunt man, is he not? Of an age and almost frail. Rather scholarly in his aspect."

I said that this was so.

"He has been seen. But I did not until now know that gentleman's name."

"Does it convey something to you?" I asked. I thought that I saw then some indication of recognition. "It is, after all, surely a most uncommon thing."

"Perhaps," the vicar said at last. "It does, I confess, bring to mind certain old stories. Old sailors' stories…"

I grasped at a fragment of half-forgotten biographical detail. "Your father was a sea-faring man, was he not?"

"Not my father," the vicar said, distracted. "My uncle Ezra… But tell me, did this guest of yours happen to mention his Christian name"

"I have heard it," I said. "At least, I have heard what he claims it to be… Victor."

"Victor Frankenstein," said Leigh-Stanley with a quiet gravity. "I think… yes, I think that was the name…" He said nothing more, but seemed lost in thought.

"Any help that you can offer," I said at length, "will be most gratefully received."

It was my expression of supplication, even pleading, which must have struck the priest most forcefully for his aspect grew still more sympathetic.

"Go on," he said. "Tell me more. Tell me all that has occurred since the arrival of this Frankenstein."

And so I did as he had asked and I began to speak in earnest. I drank more and I told him as much as I could bring to mind about the events which had occurred since the arrival of the man in the snow.

The reverend listened and he drank also, though at a slower pace than I, and, as he listened, he grew ever more thoughtful and ever more concerned. I had just reached the point at which Frankenstein had, through the medium of a note from my wife, issued a request for "materials" when the door to the inn was thrown open, accompanied by a stern breeze of cold air and, somewhat in the manner of a stage effect, a distant growl of thunder. A man stood in the doorway and cast his head about him, evidently there in search of the—

"Reverend!"

My companion looked up.

"Mr Cassell?"

The man shuffled in and, obeying the snarled instruction from the landlord to "close that door!", hurried over to us. A sinewy fellow in his middle years, I recognised him only in vague terms from the various peregrinations I had taken around Crispin Rye. I had needed to be reminded of his identity by the priest.

"This is Mr Greene," said the reverend to his new arrival.

The man glared at me. "I know who he is."

"And this," the cleric went on pleasantly to me, "is Mr Cassell, our sexton and general man of work at the church."

We nodded at each other warily.

"Can I fetch you a drink, Mr Cassell?" asked Leigh-Stanley. "It would be a pleasure to do so, especially on what promises to be so inclement an evening."

Mr Cassell wore a look of fierce exasperation. "No, Reverend. No."

"Is there something you wished to discuss then? For you most certainly have about you an air of considerable urgency."

"Reverend, it's happened again."

"Oh? And what has…" The question dried on the lips of the priest and he blanched. "Where?"

The sexton lowered his voice and looked around him. "One of the... fresher graves. A young one. By the east of the building. A plot meant, sir, for the poor."

"It's been disturbed?"

"No, sir. Not disturbed, sir. That is – not only that. Rather, I should say – desecrated."

The priest seemed still more discomfited. "You will have to show me, Mr Cassell."

He rose to his feet and glanced back at me. "Forgive me, Mr Greene but I must away. Church business, you understand." He wore now a look of something not so very far from panic. "We shall speak again soon, you and I..."

"Of course."

"You should get home yourself, Nathaniel... The storm..."

I agreed that I should yet I did not stir.

The vicar and the sexton said their goodbyes to me and hurried out back into the unwelcoming world and their half-whispered secrets.

I sat awhile and took another drink. I brooded alone and listened as the wind whipped up, as the thunder drew closer and as rain began to lash against the windowpane. And I tried my best not to make connections of the most awful kind.

- 16 -

THE RETURN OF A GRACIOUS LADY

You may be appalled, gentlemen, at what I have now to tell you. I expect you shall think very little of me. You may consider me a coward or else a slow-witted fool and I do not deny those charges. All that I can say in my defence – and it is a poor opposition indeed – is that I was, by the time I arrived home, well in my cups, having stayed at the inn for at least another hour and having taken during that period several further glasses of increasing size.

The rain had become torrential when I came home again on horseback. The Hall lay before me – in utter darkness so far as I could make out. I could barely see and, such was my condition, my first thought was that I had imagined the dark figure who hurried out of the gloom to cross my path.

I halted, the beast whinnying in protest beneath me. I lurched my way off the animal and stood unsteadily upon the ground which by now was formed chiefly of mud.

"Who is it?" I called out, shouting against the rumble and the hiss of the elements. "What do you want?"

No answer came.

I cursed myself for an inebriated dreamer and was about to return to the saddle when a voice issued from the storm. "Nathaniel!"

A woman stepped forth, cloaked and hooded, her garment sodden, the rainwater dripping from her. Too drunk to accept the truth, I peered at the lady in question.

"Nathaniel. I am here. I am real." The draper's widow. "My love."

"What are you doing?" I asked. "What do you want with me?"

"Please. Don't speak to me so."

She shivered and looked at me with such imploring urgency that no man would have resisted.

"You will catch your death," I said. "Quickly. Come inside."

She shook her head. "Not in there."

"Come on."

"In there..." She gestured towards the house. "In there is only death."

"Why do you say that?"

"My father told me so... You know that... But the dead talk to one another. They know... what is coming... We have to get away. We have to flee! Together, we will have a chance!" She stumbled forwards. "Nathaniel!"

She fell awkwardly into my arms in a swoon. I called her name.

You will have to imagine for yourselves, gentlemen, the miserable and undignified procession that followed – I, a drunkard, the lady lolling and dead-eyed in my arms, the horse trotting alongside us – for I have no wish to recall it here.

I cannot forget one detail, however: that as we approached that structure, one by one, lights appeared in every window, like something dreadful welcoming us home. Suffice to say that, when we came at last to the house, I all but dragged the widow over the threshold and into the hallway. Here she fell to the floor, as my exhausted limbs gave out. Finally, she came to. Her eyelids fluttered open.

"Welcome home, sir," said a voice from above us. Mr Tebb was standing alone at the head of the staircase, a terrible confidence in his voice and bearing.

Behind us, something scampered to the door. I heard the clank of its closing, the heavy bolt being drawn across. This was Mrs Tebb, doubtless doing her husband's bidding. I stood, swaying, and almost feverish, as Mr Tebb called above him: "They are returned now, sir!"

And then, in answer, the sounds of two pairs of feet descending the stairs towards us. With a terrible stateliness they came into view, the two of them — my wife, smiling and radiant, and by her side, the stranger, the interloper, Victor Frankenstein.

Beside me, I felt a hand claw at my shoulder. "It's him," she said. "The man my father warned me of."

Gentlemen, to my great shame and everlasting pity, that poor woman, the draper's widow was to speak no further words in this world but these.

- 17 -

A FINAL STAND

In that moment, I felt absolute despair. Four grinning faces peered down at us. The house seemed almost to pulsate with insanity and I understood that I should have heeded the warnings from the start — from the lady at my side, from the Judge, and from my own long-buried instincts.

I knew in my heart that it was too late to run yet I endeavoured to do so anyway.

"Come along," I said to the widow who was clutching on to my flank, clawing at me as though she were drowning. "We have to get away."

She groaned her assent and, in lumbering and ungainly fashion, we turned but it was too late. Mr Tebb moved sharply behind me and barred the way.

"Alice." The voice belonged to Victor Frankenstein — low, confident and even. "Who is the lady with your husband?"

"No lady, that one," said my wife in a tone edged not only with disdain but with malice. "Her name is not known to me. She has been one amongst many."

Frankenstein raked his gaze over the widow. She seemed then to be slipping into some numb and dazed condition – a fact for which I am in retrospect most grateful.

"Yet you know *what* she is," murmured our guest.

"Of course," said Alice. "Still, for all of her moral iniquities she seems to be quite healthy. There is a certain peasant's robustness to her."

"You think she will be suitable?"

Frankenstein smiled a smile of fantastic coldness. "I think she will be perfect."

I mustered a hopeless retort. "Perfect for what?"

Frankenstein raised an eyebrow, his only subtle indication of excitement. "The construction of a new human form is all but complete. We are missing a single vital component. Your arrival, just a little ahead of the worst of the storm, could scarcely be more accurate in that regard."

"What component is missing from your vile design?"

Frankenstein took no obvious pleasure in what he said next but rather spoke with all the dreadful gravity of the cultivator of science. "A human heart," he said. "The fresher the better."

I shouted some wild imprecation.

The widow groaned in half-cognisant horror. And Victor Frankenstein raised his left hand in a weird, hieratic gesture, a wordless act of appalling command.

Outside, the storm gathered all its strength. Thunder rolled mightily. Rain hurled itself against the edifice.

Inside, the worst of the nightmare began.

- 18 -
THE STORM

Gentlemen, I cannot even now face the memory of what occurred in the minutes that passed after Frankenstein gave his terrible, unspoken decree.

My mind shies away from the recollection as of that of some persistent nightmare. I remember it now not in its entirety but as a series of glimpses only, like the movement of shadows by candlelight against a darkened wall.

I remember the dull cries of the draper's widow as she was dragged from my side and pulled towards the stairs. I remember my weak, pitiful struggle with the Tebbs, who took me away. I remember Victor and Alice pulling the widow between them up to the first floor and towards that grim chamber which once in happier times had been a space meant only for merriment. I remember seeing and understanding at last precisely what it was that the monster had constructed there — a terrible workshop, a laboratory devoted to the blackest arts, a place that seethed and boiled and hissed, which palpitated, hummed and crackled. It had become a landscape of horror.

I caught sight of a figure laid out upon a slab as one might set down a cadaver — a small thing (smaller somehow than I had expected to see) and oddly incomplete.

Yet it was then but a shadow to me and not the thing that it would soon become.

Instead, my attention was drawn to what they did to the poor widow. Please, gentlemen, do not make me dwell upon her sacrifice.

Her screams echo still in my imagination. Mr Tebb held me down; I was too weak to resist him. Frankenstein took the widow in his arms while Alice soothed her as might a farmer to a kid before the slaughter.

Then I saw what my wife did next. She brought out a knife, gleaming in the surging illumination of that room and pulled it once against the young lady's throat. It was quick in the end. I do grant myself that small piece of solace.

Then the doctor set to work. He pulled at her garments to expose her chest. His lean, aged fingers swiftly found her sternum, her ribcage and what lay beneath it. I began to watch the gory extraction. I did my best, gentlemen, to at least bear witness, even as I sobbed and cried aloud in outrage and despair.

Yet I wanted to look away but my mind would not obey. Even as Victor Frankenstein pushed his hands into a blood-slick cavity of his own creation, even as he reached in to take possession of that precious organ which had been beating but moments before. Even as his face, speckled now with flecks of gore, was lit up by a smile of triumph.

At last, I felt darkness descend. I seized at it with gratitude and I surrendered to a swoon.

The last thing that I heard before I sank beneath waves of silence and merciful forgetting was high, wild, mad laughter, though I am still far from certain from whom this came.

When I awoke again it was to the sound of thunder. I found myself in the room adjacent to the ballroom. I was upright upon a chair but I was bound with cruel expertise. My mouth was gagged. Quite helpless, I could not move.

Victor Frankenstein stood over me, his face lit by cold

glee. Outside, the storm surged. Within, the visitor began to pace and to speak, to tell me secrets, and I had no alternative, gentlemen, none at all, but to listen:

- 19 -
VICTOR'S STORY

I am a more widely travelled man than you might at first assume from my manner and deportment. You have long detected a touch of the continent, I think, to my accent? In this you are correct for I am indeed not native to these shores but rather, by birth, a Genevese. My family was a distinguished one and my father a person of great nobility and wisdom. All are gone now, all passed from the earth, the name of my forebears, my father, my mother, my sister bride…

Ah, but you seem confused, my friend. You push against your restraints. Your eyes bulge with disbelief and with horror. It need not be so. You must not fight a moment longer. Please allow me to explain. For it is important to me, and to those to whom you are still dear, that you comprehend as much as you possibly can before the great work is tonight completed.

You think me a charlatan, yes? A wandering fool? A mountebank and a liar who has corrupted your wife and your servants out of nothing more than boredom and malice? A murderer too, I dare say, for what I have done to that poor and largely blameless widow. These things are all untrue, or at least they are not entirely the case.

Alice's first impressions of me were more accurate, my friend, than yours. No, I do not consider myself to be an angel or emissary (not in the sense that she believed) but I do know that I have been sent here with a purpose that is as close to divine as any man may climb.

It is not a purpose that was ever intended by God. And you and I, being men, in our different ways, of logic and of reason have both long since parted company with that old creed of the nursery. For I know precisely the thing that has sent me here and I know why it chose to do so. For I looked deep into its yellow eyes and I saw there great understanding allied to a vision which no solely human being ever might possess.

Ah, but I have confused you, have I not? I have gone too quickly and, like the little boy skimming stones across the lake, I have given mere glancing impressions of a life of rare complexity and strangeness.

I started, did I not, by speaking of my travels?

Now, let me tell you more. They began when I was but a young man and when I left my father's house for the university at Ingolstadt. Once there, I fell into company which you would no doubt consider to be unwise. I became a student of profane ideas which had, for generations, been buried and neglected. Names which I know will strike even you – a scholar of ancient lore – to be bywords for the archaic, the quaint and the dangerous. Names such as Paracelsus and Cornelius Agrippa. I fell too under the sway of one of the masters of the university: a man named Waldman whose ruthless pursuit of arcane knowledge, although it fell far short of what was needed, provided me with a certain inspiration.

Whilst studying under him I became devoted to an idea – one might rather say a dream – that of creating new life by a method which required nothing that was not already in the world. I make no apology for my beliefs for I thought then, and I still believe now, that such is within Man's grasp if he only has the wit – and, yes, Mr Greene, the daring! – to grasp it. Yes, sir. Man's. Not woman's. Not theirs alone! It is our birthright if only we can find the key. And so I did precisely that. In those Ingolstadt rooms, I did it. I created life. From a patchwork of other lives. Something new. Something great and terrible, though for so long I saw in it merely my own failures and the horrors of what came after. Only in subsequent years have I begun to perceive the true majesty of my own creation.

It was on a night, sir, not so very different to this that I first brought life into the world. When I seized it from the heavens and poured it into a vessel of my own creation. Yes, Mr Greene. Yes. Do you hear the storm surge? The rain lashing at the roof and the windowpanes? The distant roll of thunder. The promise of lightning far away. But drawing closer, sir, drawing ever closer.

The tempest approaches, Mr Greene, just as it did decades past in that foreign city. Tonight, sir, in your house in this haunted little village, history is meant to be repeated but this time I shall make no error. I will not turn aside from my creation but I will embrace it. Yes, I will be proud.

Stop struggling, Mr Greene. You cannot stop what has to happen in this house tonight. And we have but little time left to us before it begins.

The story of my youth is an old one and I have told it before. I have spoken of that Creature whom I formed from the elements. I have spoken of how it turned its face from me. I have spoken of how it set out to destroy every good thing that ever I loved. How it killed my little brother, my maidservant, my father, my best friend and, last of all, she who had mere hours before consented to become my wife. It was a bloody campaign of revenge which spanned continents and years.

In the end, I had no choice but to track down he who had dedicated himself to my destruction. We set out together, a chase without purpose or seeming end. It took us from Geneva and it finished at the very ends of the earth itself. Yes, well-travelled I have been and I thought once that I was even to meet my death in the wastes of the Arctic itself, deep in the hectares of ice.

Ah. The ice. The great expanse of it. That was where my long pursuit of the Creature ended, or, rather, where it seemed to end. I became lost and was rescued by a vessel under the command of a most excellent Englishman by the name of Robert Walton. He cared for me, healed me and heard my tale. At the end of it, my Creature clambered aboard the ship – for his strength is more than human and his resourcefulness is that of the very Devil himself – in order to confront me for what I believe we both took to be a final time. There were terrible words that we exchanged and he left me there to die. He himself was last witnessed leaping into great fields of white where he was soon lost to darkness and distance.

This, at least, was the official account as given by Walton to certain interested authorities after he returned home. The truth was not so dramatic. I have not time now to detail the particulars but a deal was struck with that wise and learned sea captain – that he would lie about my death and that he would stay silent in exchange for what was left of my inheritance.

I see that you strain still at your bonds, Mr Greene. Please, sir, I would advise against it for what is to take place cannot now be diverted or undone. The moment is almost upon us. The storm soars outside. Perhaps you can hear also the noises of my machines? The seething, crackling, bubbling of those instruments which I have placed in the grandest room of this little mansion? Do you feel intruded upon, sir? Do you feel as though I have taken liberties? You have my apologies, Mr Greene, you really do – though I wonder if you might not yet be pleased and happy with the consequence of it all.

And so I returned to England with Mr Walton. The crew were paid off. I gave Walton all that I had and, believing my Creature at long last to be altogether lost to the wildest reaches of the globe, I intended to go back to my work, to those great labours of my life.

For a time I experienced some small success in this regard. In the anonymous belly of the city of London I was able to earn a living of the most modest sort as a tutor and, in my hours of leisure, to look once again into charnel houses and into potter's fields, to enquire into the habits of medical students and to let it be known to certain quarters of the underworld that I was always in search of fresh cadavers. Any former doubts I had about the wisdom of my work I had long since set aside.

I began work on the construction of a new and better Creature but I was in this ambition soon thwarted. Walton's sailors were not beings of utmost discretion as they had claimed but rather men whose tongues could easily be loosened by the application of liquor, money or simple boredom. There was something of a scandal made. Wild tales with only the slimmest foundation in reality began to spread. A mob was soon whipped up, and I was discovered in the midst of the creation of my art.

I fought but events had weakened me to the point that my

capture was a simple matter. There was no trial of any kind and my activities were not made public. Yet neither was there an execution and I expect I should be grateful for that, though my captors were in every other sense moral and scientific pygmies.

For years, my dear Mr Greene, I was taken from the waking world and imprisoned. They called them asylums – for I spent time in many of them – though in truth they were nothing more than rough gaols. I was given a number rather than a name and I was locked up from all that I once had known.

How long? How long did I spend in institutions? I can see your beseeching eyes asking me that question. I cannot say for certain. Yet decades have passed, I have no doubt. Decades!

My greatest enemy in those places was an absolute lack of mental excitation. No-one was my peer and the doctors were all idiots, each new cure of theirs more ludicrous than the last. I do believe that after a while they took to giving me certain medicaments mixed in with my food for I found myself oftentimes becoming drowsy for many of the daylight hours. You yourself now know something of the efficacy of this method. My existence shrank to a succession of walls and padlocks, my only exercise a ragged patch of grass.

These are years – wasted years, Mr Greene! – on which I do not care now to dwell. For they were long, unprofitable, stale, wretched things, as of some fitful and unhappy sleep from which I was quite unable to awake. Unable that is – until the great interruption arrived. A day in that purgatory which saw an incredible arrival, a sight which I thought never to have seen again, one which would set me on a fresh path and which would send me, Mr Greene, to your door and to that of your wife. I, the only man who could give you both your heart's desire!

But hark! The thunder grows louder! The storm is almost at its zenith. There is more – much more – to tell but I must away for the time of the experiment is nigh and the midnight hour is upon us! Wait, Mr Greene. Wait and behold a miracle, sir, and all, I give you my word, all will yet be well!

- 20 -
THE ARRIVAL

With these words, my uninvited guest ran pell-mell from the chamber. He made no effort to free me or even to loosen my restraints.

The tempest outside was full of sound and fury. The house seemed to shake with it. From the room next door I heard a dreadful cacophony of noises, rising even above the roar of thunder. I heard first a deep sound, that of some weird mechanism. I heard the shouted commands of Victor Frankenstein and the cringing, cur-like replies of the servants. I heard a crackling and a fizzing sound. I heard a terrible wrenching noise. I heard the pitiful scream of my wife.

I struggled, fruitlessly, against my bonds. The storm grew louder still and I had no doubt now that it was directly above the house itself. Then, with a sort of inevitable poetry, there was the sound of something crashing in the room beside me. A terrible smell of burning. A shriek, the sounds of struggle and then something quite impossible: the sound of a voice that I had never heard in all the world before.

If things had until that point seemed chaotic, now came utter pandemonium. Still unable to move, I could do nothing but listen. I heard cries, shouts, lamentations, the sound of boots upon the floor, the noise of running and panic. I could make out few words but I heard my wife shout: "Keep it away!" and the voice of the architect of our downfall, raised in outrage and fury: "But this is what you wanted! This is what you begged me for!"

"But not," she said, "like this! Not this blasphemy... Dear God, its eyes!"

Against this commotion I was finally able to begin to free myself. I fought against the bonds and struck the feet of the chair hard against the floor, confident I would not be disturbed. At last, I heard the splintering of wood. I smashed down the chair again and felt one of its legs give way. Spurred on by this success, I began to work the gag out of my mouth, pushing it out and down towards my chin. It was wickedly slow going, an act of utter desperation.

So caught up was I in my efforts that I did not realise for some minutes how quiet it had become outside. The storm had passed over, though the rain kept up its ferocious drumming. Yet I could hear no sounds of human activity, no voices raised or movement.

Aside from the rain, I could hear only my own ragged panting, the product of my frantic labours. With one final smash of the chair upon the wall I got free my left hand and then my right. It was the work of mere minutes after that to loosen the remainders of my bonds. At last, bruised and aching, I stood in that antechamber a free man.

I listened but heard nothing except precipitation. I felt quite sure somehow that my wife, the servants and Frankenstein himself had fled the house and left me all alone. Or, rather, not quite alone for I heard then a sound quite unmistakable – the small, shuffling footsteps of a child.

"Hello?" I called out. "Who goes there?"

The footsteps came near to the very door. I stepped closer, reached for the handle, then hesitated for I knew with a chill certainty that whatever stood beyond the partition was not in the strictest sense a human being at all.

I paused, uncertain if I could face another unholy sight – the selfsame sight which had chased away all the rest. For an instant, I wished only for oblivion, even, perhaps for the oblivion of death.

Then I saw the handle be depressed, but fumblingly and without expertise. It happened again yet the door did not open. I watched in a state of appalled paralysis. At the third attempt, the door opened. It swung forwards and I saw a silhouette upon the threshold.

It was small and rather crooked in aspect. Had he been a natural human being he would have looked around six or seven years of age. His body was criss-crossed with livid scars and looping stitching. His skin was as parchment and his eyes were a dreadful shade of yellow. His face was squat and malformed. Yet did that unnatural little being raise a hand in greeting. A smile of babyish innocence lit up his dwarfish face and in that moment of seeing, gentlemen, I felt a new emotion, an emotion so pure and fierce in its intensity that I realised I had experienced before only its dimmest shadow. It was an emotion which all but felled me as I stood there, in that nightmare room in that nightmare house, and the name of that emotion, sirs, was *love*.

PART FOUR

THE PERSONAL TESTIMONY OF JESSE MALONE

(continued)

I

No sooner had the condemned man spoken the word "love" than his narrative was interrupted by a great rattling and clanging sound from behind us.

So engrossed had I become in his weird tale, that the squalid surroundings of that cell had receded somewhat in my imagination, and it was a rude awakening indeed to be reminded of them. Even my headache had been, to some degree, allayed by the ponderous rhythm of Greene's words.

The door, unlocked now, was opened and two figures stepped in. The first was the gaoler, and, at his side, the priest from Crispin Rye, the Reverend Leigh-Stanley.

At the sight of us, the preacher seemed utterly astonished.

"Reverend!" Greene said, and he seemed to be touched indeed at the visitation. "Thank you so much for coming."

I realised now that, in the case of Leigh-Stanley, it was no mere surprise on his face but something more like horror.

He backed away, looking feverishly first at us and then the prisoner. "I'm sorry," he said, failing visibly to control himself. "Dear God, but I am so sorry…"

"Reverend," Greene began. "Please, I…"

Yet he said nothing further for the priest turned and left, all but running from the room.

"Sir, wait!" the gaoler called. "Wait for me out there!" Swiftly, the fellow turned back to us. "And you two are done now as well. That's enough. Enough for today."

Mr Crowe started to protest. "I don't believe that the

prisoner had finished his account. Surely, there's a good deal more to tell and to be heard?"

"Your audience is over," said the official with the firmness of a schoolmaster with a child. "Now, please, gentlemen. Walk with me."

II

I could see from the face of my friend that he was frustrated by the thought we might not hear the remainder of the condemned man's story on that long, hot afternoon but might instead be forced to wait until such time as the prison authorities granted us entrance once again.

He turned to the guard and relaxed his features into an expression which suggested a kind of open, reasonable generosity of spirit, one which had, in the past, worked upon even the most closed and determined of minds.

On the guard, however, this performance failed entirely to work its magic.

"I have my orders, sir," he said, and I noticed that he possessed the boldness to look my friend clear in the eye. "The prisoner is not to be questioned any further. The interview is done with for today."

Crowe looked downcast. "And nothing can be said to change the mind of the men in charge?"

"Nothing, sir," said the guard, his tone flat and without the possibility of compromise. I looked at the gaoler then, perhaps truly noticing him for the first time. He was younger than I had first assumed, though I saw that his hair had turned grey prematurely. His face bore the lineaments of he who had been born with a considerable quantity of natural beauty but from whom the travails of a hard life had extracted a steep price. His nose was crooked and suggested to me also that he drank a little more than was wise. "Now you had better follow me, gentlemen, or else suffer yourselves to be removed."

Neither of us stirred.

The guard shook his head. "It would be ungentlemanly, sirs," he said. "Undignified." He looked me full in the eye now. "And rough."

Behind us, the man who was sentenced to hang let out a long, theatrical breath. "You had better do as you are asked," said Nathaniel Greene. "We will continue this another day, before... well..."

The implication hung heavy between us.

"So tomorrow, then?" Crowe asked hopefully.

"Maybe, sir," said the guard, "maybe. But for now – this way now."

The voice of the condemned man sounded tired. "Goodbye, Mr Crowe. Mr Malone. We shall meet again."

We agreed that we should, and we went reluctantly to the door. Once there, Mr Greene called out to us again.

"Gentlemen!"

"Yes?" I said, perhaps a little impatiently for I was eager now for the day to be done with.

"Be careful," he said.

"Of what?" I asked.

"Of the house," he said. "Of the Genevese physician, and of the tall man also. In a way he is the most terrible of any of them..."

Before we could ask more, the guard hurried us out of the door and closed it behind us. We heard the grind of the key in the lock, echoing all along that place of incarceration. Then we were out again beside the dripping walls and breathing in the foul air of the corridor.

The effect was like waking from one nightmare into another. Back we walked along the long line of cells, each one containing the worst of humanity, penned in misery. Then, as is sometimes the way, even in such a place of dread as that, we reached a moment of still quiet, in a kind of vestibule which lay beyond the last of the cells and the start of the outer workings of the prison, that plethora of walls and gateways which would lead us, in painstaking stages, back out into the world beyond.

Our keeper stopped short. He turned, held up a hand and looked searchingly at us. He glanced first left, then right, and saw that we were to be undisturbed at least for a minute or two. He cleared his throat.

What he said then was a source of great surprise to me. It was, on the face of it, a weird coincidence though I am starting now to wonder whether coincidence as we tend to understand it quite exists in this black and deadly business.

"Gentlemen," he said, and I heard now a note of the countryside in his accent. "I must tell you that man, the devil in the cell has yet to recognise me. But I can tell you that some at least of what he has said is nothing but the sheer gospel truth."

"However can you say so?" I asked.

Crowe, meanwhile, was gazing at the fellow as though he represented something vital and hitherto overlooked.

"You were at the Hall?" Crowe asked, although it was a question which sounded more like a statement to me.

The gaoler nodded. "I was one of the Judge's men. I came that day for the money and for the fun of it. He promised us all the chance for a bit of rough and tumble. But nothing hard. No real difficulties."

Crowe's eyes were trained upon the gaoler. "But you didn't want to go, then? Deep down?"

"No, sir, I did not."

"May I ask why?"

The gaoler met the gaze of my friend. "I think you know why, sir."

Crowe gave a single, curt nod. Somewhere behind us I heard the great iron clang of a door slamming shut.

"It's the house, isn't it?" Crowe murmured. "Fieldwick Hall itself?"

The guard lowered his head. "Always something about that place, sir. Stories. Things seen. Something I glimpsed myself, sir, once or twice… On a dare, with the other boys from the village…"

There came another clanging sound. Then the sound of hurrying, rather martial footsteps.

"I don't want to say any more," said our new acquaintance, nervous now. "I don't believe I'm able to."

A key rattled loudly in the lock of the door behind us.

And the guard said only this: "Whatever they did in the Hall, sir, whatever was made there… it would have been rendered a hundred times more terrible because of the nature of that place."

Then the door opened up behind us and another guard emerged. He looked at us with surprise.

"Got to keep going, Mr Briggs!" he said, in the firm, commanding voice of the parade ground.

Our own guide nodded and said that he would do so, and all four of us went through the next door and out into the labyrinth beyond. The other man stalked away, not without giving our party a look of marked suspicion.

"Will you come with us?" Mr Crowe asked our man.

He shook his head. "I don't care to, sir, and besides my duties are many. But I would, sir, if you'll let me, like to give you one piece of advice—"

The voice of my friend, a jagged thing now, cut across the little speech, which had been delivered with a sort of sweet hesitation. "Not if you are to tell me to stay away from Fieldwick Hall," he said. "Not if you are simply to serve me up with spook stories and superstition."

This description struck me as being altogether unfair given the profession of he who spoke it but the gaoler seemed both unoffended and oddly unsurprised.

The man gave us a slow, sad smile. "Good luck, sirs," he said. "Good luck to both of you."

After that no more of substance was said and he led us out into the free world. I thought he might say more on the very threshold of the prison, but he simply bade us a good afternoon and closed the door behind us.

When I turned to Hubert Crowe, I saw, to my horror, that he was beaming, a dreadful, uncharacteristic grin disturbing his ordinary features. At the sight of him, an odd phrase from scripture burst unbidden into my mind, a line from the first gospel: "and his face did shine like the sun".

III

I meant to find a cab to bear me home to Clerkenwell but Crowe wished to walk awhile, through the torrid city. In the wretched heat, my headache doubled itself, then doubled again.

"Do you want to know?" Crowe asked. "Know how Greene's story ended?"

"I'm curious," I said, and this was true enough. "Of course."

"Then I shall seek another audience. Tomorrow if I can. Time, I fear, is not our friend in this matter."

I touched my right temple and winced. "Send me word," I said. "I will come with you to hear whatever there is to hear."

Crowe smiled, in a normal fashion this time, and, for an instant he seemed himself again. "Till tomorrow then."

"Tomorrow."

A look of tentative hope crossed his pale, unremarkable face.

"Thank you," he said simply.

Yet I was not to see my friend again for many long days after this conversation and by then he had been changed utterly.

IV

I went home and I lay in a darkened room awhile till the headache passed. I tried not to think too hard about the awful gravity of Crispin Rye nor of the uncanny connections that it seemed to breed. I did my best to sleep and to recover and to beat away that grim and grasping fear which assailed me. I even prayed, once or twice, and asked for better things to come.

The next morning, though my headache had departed, brought no word from Crowe. Only in the afternoon did a scrawled message arrive, delivered to Mrs Armitage by a vagabond child. It was composed of a handful of lines:

> Prison has barred any further visits to Greene.
> Suspect high-up interference. Will appeal and
> achieve all I can. Anything that you can do by
> means of the Assembly would be much appreciated.
> He has four days left to him.

Away from the persuasiveness of the man in the prison cell, the allure of his tale had ebbed from me. I sensed that Crowe's own obsession might be lessened if it received no further sustenance. And so I did nothing to arrange any further visit to Newgate. The city still sweated and stank and so I stayed home and waited for news. I considered writing but did not. I tried not to fret unduly and I failed in that too. I barely stirred from bed. The following day there came another note from Crowe:

> Still nothing. And no way in.
> I grow desperate to learn the truth.

I thought I saw the signs of his fascination reaching a fever-pitch, a thing that gave me hope that the fever in question might be about to break. Mrs Armitage asked me if all was quite well. I sensed that she was concerned at my seclusion. I told her that I was fine and that I hoped some improvement might even be imminent. In this I spoke no lie.

Then, on the third day, I received not a message but a letter, a most long and detailed letter, and one which came not from Hubert Crowe but from a different source entirely. I will paste it all into this scrapbook so that you might see. Yes? So that you might understand.

I will preface it also with three other documents which I have found since then and which, I do believe, cast further light on the whole dark business. It is the chronology, I think, which proves the truth of the links in the chain.

Do you yourself begin to see it now, I wonder, as I do? The whole and dreadful pattern of it?

PART FIVE

THREE FURTHER SIGHTINGS

I

Document found by authorities in the house of Alfred Ferrars of Ketchering, Suffolk, upon the day of his transportation to Australia[*]

I never believed in ghosts or spirits or in Things From the Underworld or in anything at all of that sort. I have never written down any part of my life neither. And I would not be doing it now except that it seems important somehow, and I think if I do not put down what happened here then I will wake in the morning and think it all a dream or worse.

It happened in the Woods, deep in the heart of them, in the quietest, stillest part where few if any of them round here ever dares to tread. But I am safe, or I always thought I was. For my father, in spite of what the gossips and the sharp-tongued old women say, my father was a decent man, a man of honour and knowledge. He taught me well before his passing all the secrets of the woodland, all the hidden pathways, all the safe places

---

[*] The transportation itself took place the July of 1850. I suspect that this decidedly odd memorandum was written in the January of that year.

and the many traps, all the ways to stay alive out amongst the trees.

I care not what my ma said of him either as she lay dying, raving about his mistakes and how he let her down. He was always a good father to me, and I believe I owe my life to him, many times over. But now, after tonight, I owe my life to another too.

I should have seen it, hidden among the branches of the old oak tree – that vicious piece of machinery, that iron foothold trap, which had been left there (I have no doubt) by Old Caterham, who owns these woods and much around them, at least according to battles that were fought and won near a thousand years past, not long after the Conqueror came. If this is to be a record then let it show that the Caterhams are violent and greedy men and always have been, for as far back as anyone can remember, men who don't know how to share and men who don't care to learn the trick of it neither.

But that is all as maybe. My point stands that I know it was one of old Caterham's men that would have hid the wicked thing in that place – most likely Grigson, a gamekeeper with ideas far above his station and who married poor Annie Ling, may God rot his blackened soul.

Yes, Grigson would be my bet, doing it on Caterham's orders. I can just see the pair of them chuckling at the thought of harming a hard-working man like me.

Though I blame myself for what happened and for blundering into the trap, my head full in fact of fair Annie and of how we had left matters between us when we parted.

The trap was savage as it closed upon my leg, and I swore and cried and wept as it got me. I went down hard, and lay wounded in the earth, screaming in the midst of a wood where no other man would hear me, save for he who set the trap in the first place.

As I lay on the ground, blood pouring from my leg and my head, I drifted into dreamland. I thought I saw my father, my mother, the face of a smiling stranger, the giggle of a child, all of it nonsense I promise you for a man can imagine some queer things I've no doubt when he lies dying.

And I might have died. I have to be honest about that. Blood was flowing, I could not move and there are many creatures in the woods who would have liked the taste of it. Even as I lay there I believed I could hear a few of them rustling through the undergrowth, coming closer, wanting a better look.

Oh, I tried to get the thing off my leg. But it couldn't be done. I didn't have the strength. No man alone could have done it. Or so I thought.

I know I keep circling about the truth of it, of what I saw in the woods, of the thing that saved me. I will write it down and let folks think what they want.

But as I lay upon the forest floor, listening to what sounded like the tramp of a beast moving closer to me (I thought perhaps it was a wild pig though it sounded too heavy for that) I saw a man lurch into view, an impossible one, a person more than seven feet high. He moved like none I have ever seen before, and he showed impossible strength, for he pulled the trap away from my leg and lifted me free like I was as light as tidewood. He bore me away in his arms after, like some big, swollen baby.

He took me home, though I cannot remember the long walk and he must have laid me in my bed and given me strong drink and some medicaments. In part an apothecary, in part a spirit of the forest, in part a giant whose deep eyes spoke of old knowledge. You will think I dreamed him, though I did not. You will think I freed myself somehow and just stumbled home in some sort of fever.

Yet I know in my heart I did not and besides I have proof: the rough, jagged stitches in my leg placed there while I lay in liquored slumber and which I know now most certainly saved my life.

II

∽∾∽

Correspondence between Nicholas Amberson
and his mother, Cornelia Amberson

3RD JANUARY, 1850

Dear Mother,

I understand that this will not be a welcome letter for you to receive nor shall it be an easy thing to read. Nonetheless, I would ask you, cordially and with no small amount of love, to read what I have written, to try to understand my actions and even, perhaps, should God will it, for you to find it in your heart some measure of happiness for me and pride in yourself for the son whom you brought up all but single-handedly.

Now, let me get to the nub of it. This morning, shortly before noon, I made Jessica my wife.

I have not the least intention of rehearsing here once again your own ardent objections to the lady, to her initial station in life, to the uncertainty around several aspects of her parentage and to the simple fact that she is already a mother (little Sara being now dear indeed to me, an infant whom I intend to raise as my own with all the benefits and preferments which this entails). Naturally enough, we intend to make for her a host of brothers and sisters and build a family of quite considerable size.

This news will, I know, bring you little joy and may even upon initial receipt of it cause a quantity of personal pain. For this I feel nothing but regret and sadness, emotions eclipsed only by my sorrow that you could not have been at the church this morning to see us wed and to give us your blessing.

It was a small, very private ceremony, Mother. Waterman was my best man — you will remember him from school? — and there were but a few of our friends in attendance. The minister (for I know you will be curious as to who could possibly have presided over so scandalous a union) was the Reverend P R Wherry.

He showed us nothing but kindness and I honestly believe that the great majority of the rumours about him must be entirely false and without basis. His interpretations of scripture are, at worst, nothing more than eccentric and the company that he keeps in his hours of leisure is surely a matter for him and his Creator. It is also the truth (for have I not always striven with you to be honest at all times?) that he was the only holy man in all of London who would agree to sanctifying the match.

Still, it is done now and we are both delirious with joy. We are spending our wedding night in a small hotel in the west of the city (you will understand, I am sure, if I am no more precise than that) and tomorrow we are to embark upon a short but hopefully most agreeable honeymoon.

Little Sara is to stay with her aunt for the duration of our trip.

You will approve of our destination, I hope – we are to journey to the east of the nation, to the county of Suffolk and its fenlands, that portion of the world from which your own ancestors hailed. We will be away for no more than two weeks. I wish to see some churches of interest and Jessica hopes to paint some of that region's distinctive landscape. (Ah, but you did not know that she painted, did you? Her talent is still budding but it is appreciable.)

Upon our return, Mother, it is my dearest wish that we be reconciled and that you take my Jessica to your bosom at last. I know that this is improbable indeed but do the gospels not teach us that miracles are possible with a sufficient application of faith?

I must go now, Mother. My bride awaits.

Though I remain, your most loving son, Nicholas

10TH JANUARY, 1850

My darling boy,

Firstly, I hope that this message reaches you safely and soon. Since you had neglected to leave for me any address at which you might be reached, I had to send this first to your friend Waterman in the hope that he will see it reaches your hands.

He always was a polite, well-behaved boy, coming from such good stock, and I hope sincerely that he will obey my request in this matter.

Secondly, thank you for relaying to me the news of your marriage. You were quite correct in some of your assumptions concerning my sentiments about the matter. In others, however, I may yet surprise you, and, I hope, please you also.

I have sat with your tidings, Nicholas, and I have spoken with God about it and I have, with His guidance, chosen a path, if not of approval then at least of acceptance. To practise charity is the greatest commandment of the gospels and I have perhaps been too meagre in my provision of this quality to she who is now "Mrs Amberson". The task will not be an easy one, but I mean to set my shoulder to the wheel in order to welcome both her and her child to our family. It is my dearest wish that we meet on cheerful terms when you return to London.

Thirdly, and finally, I am delighted at your choice for your honeymoon tour! As you know, that part of England lives forever in my soul and I am so pleased that something in it evidently calls also to you. What does your bride make of the region? I shall be so interested to find out.

If you receive this in time do please consider visiting the little village of Callister's Bourne, nine miles north of Ely. It was always was such a favourite of mine when I was a girl – a dear, quaint, little place with such welcoming folk. The inn, as I recall, was especially comforting and accommodating.

Thank you again. You have been true to yourself and there is much of which to be proud in that.

Do kiss that new wife of yours from me. I do so hope to see you in London again soon.

With love,
Your mother

12TH JANUARY, 1850

Dear Mother,

Oh, but I have read your letter so many times now! To Jessica's fond amusement, I keep it beside our bed so that I may read it as soon as I wake, so that I might reassure myself it is a true thing and not merely some wishful figment of my sleeping imagination. I have all but committed it to memory, every line, for it has filled me up with joy. Our honeymoon is memorable indeed, but I can hardly wait to return to London, and to your bosom, so glad am I to read of the softening of your heart and so eager am I for all four of us to be together.

Jessica also sends her warm regards.

We passed yesterday through the town of Ipswich, on we go now, into the east and to all its quiet and solemn mysteries. There shall be more soon from me.

Your loving son,
N

14TH JANUARY, 1850

Dear Mother,

Greetings from Callister's Bourne!

I am not sure whether you received my last letter. I am impatient, Mother, for word from you.

Nonetheless, I felt moved to write again almost at once for Jessica and I have changed our plans in order to accommodate your recommendation and we are come to that little village of which you spoke in your letter. It is indeed a charming place, nestled at the edge of dense woodland, a little outpost of progress against the trees.

It has an air of great tranquillity and the people, if not precisely welcoming, are most probably kind-hearted and loyal. Having visited the church this afternoon, we have secured accommodation at the inn (which has, I believe, changed its name in recent years – formerly The Bull and Baker it is now, The Trumpet and the Seal) and we mean there to raise a glass to you.

Nicholas

P.S. I write this late as my beloved drowses beside me. What a queer place this is! Did you truly mean to send us here? I can only imagine that it has changed grievously since you were ever a visitor. I have tried my best but facts must be faced. The innkeeper is unfriendly, our room is dirty and uncomfortable, the food abominable. Worse by far than those is the dread atmosphere of the place. Merely quiet in the daytime it becomes, after nightfall, filled up with menace.

The people stare at us with outright hostility and with something else (something I like even less) when they gaze upon Jessica. There is no lock upon the door to our chamber. I am certain that our travelling bags have been searched. There are footsteps outside our door and hushed voices in the night.

Something has gone grievously awry in Callister's Bourne, Mother. And so I mean to sit up this long night and to leave tomorrow with the dawn.

15TH JANUARY, 1850

Dear Mother,

I fear I must ask you to destroy my last letter to you and, if you have read it, to forget all of its contents. I know now that I cannot have been in my perfect mind when I wrote those words. They spoke, I think, of the illness that has now overtaken us. The landlord – gruff but kindly Mr Barrington – has been most obliging and has allowed us to stay for three more nights in his cosy establishment. I have been most out of sorts and have slept much yet he has kept me sustained with plentiful quantities of rich, delicious soup.

Poor Jessica seems also to be afflicted though her disorder seems to be of a subtly different hue. Dear Mr Barrington has placed her in a separate room to mine.

At first, I did not care for the notion but the landlord has assured me, over and over, that it is for the best.

How fortunate we are to have fetched up here just at the very moment of our mutual illness. How grateful are we both to you, Mother, for sending us to this kind and Christian haven!

An oddity to finish with for I am very tired. This little room of mine affords me an excellent view of the woodland. I just witnessed from my window a most extraordinary thing: a man standing at the edge of the trees looking over in the direction of the village. It must, I am sure, have been a trick of the light or else some consequence of my ailment but he seemed to me to be a veritable giant – at least seven feet in height if not more. No doubt imagined but I thought the vision might amuse you.

With love,
N

―⚋―

?*

Mother, why have you not written? You know where I am to be found. Here, still here, in Callister's Bourne. I know not how many hours and days and weeks have passed. Something has been done to us. Something in the food and drink. I spit it out when they are not looking.

My poor Jessica, what is being done to her? This is intolerable. Intolerable. I dare not write my suspicions down on paper. Too terrible. Too terrible.

I have only this brief opportunity to write as they are all distracted here – exchanging tales of a stranger living wild in the woods. I cannot, cannot think of it – the horror of what has been done to us.

Oh Mother, I have not seen Jessica for so long now.

And I no longer hear her cries.

Mother? How did you know of this place? How can you have sent us here? How can you bear to think of where you have led us?

―⚋―

---

* The precise date is uncertain but it must have been composed at a later date in January

?*

Dear Mrs Amberson,

This is not your son. I have no name for my Creator did not grant me one. I am but a stranger who chanced to be passing by this vile and benighted village on my way to conduct some necessary business of my own, some fifty miles hence, in the neighbouring county.

I write to inform you of the five following facts:

1. Callister's Bourne is all aflame and will shortly be mere ashes.
2. Its people are scattered or dead. I know not what has corrupted them to this extent nor do I care to find out.
3. I fear very much that the mind of your son has been broken.
4. She who has the great misfortune to be your daughter-in-law yet lives and her heart cries out for vengeance.
5. I have encountered a great deal of what men call evil in my long and strange existence yet you – you, Mrs Amberson – may yet prove to be the very worst. I have long wrestled with the possible existence or otherwise of a deity; you would seem offer only further evidence for the impossibility of a loving God.

I humbly suggest, madam, that you set whatever affairs you have in order.

Yours,
A Stranger

---

* Again, no date is given here but it must originate from late January of the same year, given the Creature's movements at that time

FROM THE ANNOUNCEMENTS, DEATHS COLUMN OF *THE TIMES*, FEBRUARY 14TH, 1850

AMBERSON, CORNELIA

Sad to relate, this good Christian woman is to be laid in the ground this Sunday hence.

Her passing was sudden and unexpected and leaves her family grieving. She is survived by her son (at present, overseas), her daughter-in-law Jessica and a granddaughter, Sara.

The funeral will be a private affair.

III

∽o∽

A letter found in the possession of "Elias",
an aged vagrant of the city of Norwich,
upon his thirteenth arrest for begging*

To the blind gentleman who was kind
to me, in a spot by the ruined Wall.

My dear sir,

I trust that you will find this letter, nestled amongst your meagre belongings, in the spot where you sleep by the remnants of the medieval wall which surrounds this ancient city. I tucked it out of sight of unfriendly eyes and secreted it as best I could from the ravages of the elements. I expect you shall be surprised upon its discovery, but it is my sincere hope that the surprise will be of the pleasantest sort. I hope too that you may find a friend who can read this to you aloud.

I have travelled much, seen a good deal of the wide world and in that time I have encountered many instances of wickedness and sin, amongst the most parlous of which I chanced

---

* Again, the composition of this letter must be late January in 1850.

upon just lately. It grieves me to admit that examples of true goodness have been far rarer, though you, good sir, and your generous conduct number high amongst them.

You heard my approach, sir, you heard how I was cold and tired and hungry. Yet you did not spurn me but invited me in to your humble, makeshift dwelling (the removal of which I know you fear daily at the hands of the authorities). You gave me food and let me sleep and asked for nothing in return.

It is as pure a moment of charity as I am able to recall. I thank you, sir, from the bottom of my heart. This morning I woke early and I had to press on, for my business is of an urgent sort but I wished to spend just a few moments in the composition of this letter, in gratitude for your kindness. Last night you asked me to tell you something of my life and I was happy to do so. You listened with patient sincerity even at its most peculiar contortions. Yet there was more to say. We were both of us tired and in need of rest. You asked in particular what became of my maker and whether I met him again, after our long and terrible chase across the ice. So let me tell you now, sir, before I bid farewell, how I came to see that evil wretch once more and how I permitted myself to be gulled into making an error of the most appalling kind.

We last we met amid the Arctic tundra. I believed him dead. There are those who say that I killed my own maker, though this is not so. At the sight of me, he gave a terrific cry of pain and despair then fell silent.

I went to him and found no signs of life and breath. At this realisation, I felt a kind of anguished relief and flung myself into the freezing waters before I could be discovered by that crew of desperate mariners.

I thought then to lose myself in lonely exile, an orphan, an outcast and a creature unique in all the annals of humanity. I have come since to supersede such feelings of self-pity but such were my emotions at the time.

Alone in that icy wasteland, I soon learned how to survive and – more than that – I learned also how to take pleasure in my survival. Years passed in that place – even now I am uncertain as to quite how many – and in that time I discovered much of myself and of the nature of the universe. It was a hermit's life that I led, and I had time to consider all that had befallen me and to examine also the sundry connections that exist between all living things. In that land of pure isolation I came, through deep contemplation, to rise above that dull rage which had been at my back since the very moment of my spurning, and to find a kind of peaceful wisdom in solitude and thought.

Even the moment of my own creation which I had long considered to be an aberration and a perversity, I came in those long days and nights of cold to see as merely a different element of a vast design, a new part of a greater pattern. In these thoughts, I found a measure of comfort – at least until the dreams began.

They started as mere glimpses to interrupt my slumber – of my maker, not as he had once been, a young student of medicine with a noble countenance and shining eyes but as an older man, growing bent and careworn.

I know not whether you would set store or not by such visions, my friend, though I at first did not, thinking them the product of imagination and perhaps of too long being spent away from the world of man. Though as the dreams went on, visiting me with ever greater regularity and growing in detail and duration, I began to wonder if there might not exist between Victor Frankenstein and I some unknown correlation, and also whether I might have assumed his demise in error.

As time went by, this thought became a suspicion and that suspicion as close to a certainty as was possible. In this fashion, I made up my mind to leave my home of snowy exile and return to the world of the everyday. The journey was long and arduous. I walked first to the edge of the ice. I stowed away awhile on board a vessel, the drunken captain of which wore a face I knew of old. I wandered through the country of England and found more changed since last I had journeyed through the great cities of Europe.

Bad dreams dogged me all the while.

I came to London – a great, bustling city of the future – and there I slumbered a while in order to restore my strength. Upon my being woken once again I set to work in earnest in the pursuit and discovery of he who once had birthed me: Victor Frankenstein.

I will not trouble you with an account of all those many archives and offices of records which I consulted, in secret and under cover of darkness, before I learned the truth about my maker. Suffice it to say that there were many such nocturnal consultations (in which I was always careful to disguise my handiwork so that no evidence of my presence there would ever be discovered) before I found his whereabouts.

The trail was there for those who could recognise the links between incidents which would strike the layman as being without connection. In this fashion, I pieced together his movements in the years of our separation. That he survived the ice was clear enough as was his subsequent voyage to England (no doubt using all those means and wiles which lie at his disposal to purchase and ensure the silence of the crew). Then there was a return to his old activities as might an opium eater go back over and again to the habit. He swore that he was done with his dreams of creation but I always suspected him to be lying, to himself as well as to others. Then came his arrest (under an assumed name) then his trial and incarceration in the first of a series of madhouses. He seems to have been moved with some regularity between such institutions. I do not know the precise reason for this though I have come to harbour a suspicion – that in spite of my maker's use of an alias, there were those in authority who knew of his true identity and who ensured that he was not kept in any single place for too great a length of time, lest his secret be discovered.

From London to Exeter to Devon, I followed his trail through the archives, and from there to Cornwall and Lincolnshire before finding what I took to be his most recent abode, penned up amongst the lunatics, in an asylum in the county of Norfolk some twenty miles from this very city and near a certain village by the name of Crispin Rye.

It was to this place that I set out then in the January of 1843. This country is not my own – for I was born, if such you can call it, in the city of Ingolstadt, an ocean away from here, and I found much about this kingdom to be strange.

My journey from London into the depths of the English countryside had more incident and peril for it is hard for me to travel unnoticed and without attracting attention of the most unwelcome sort.

Needless for now to say that I pressed on and reached at last that terrible place in which my creator was imprisoned. Many times I was tempted to turn back but on I went. For the dreams had become by then insistent things indeed.

The asylum was situated in a place of great emptiness. It once had been a farmhouse and it was surrounded by fields and woodland. It was supposed, I think, by those in charge that this proximity to nature would soothe the wild and troubled souls who dwelt within its stone walls.

The place was easy enough to approach and I watched it from the shadows for a day and a night before I slunk inside, beneath the fences that stood at its perimeter and into its hallways by means of a foolishly unlocked door, in the early hours of the morning. The institution was neither well-ordered or well run. My long hours of observation had made this plain to me. I found my way to the cell of my maker and I watched through the bars as he slept.

Soon enough, my presence woke him. He blinked, stared, rose from his wretched cot and walked over to where I stood, his movements like those of a man in a dream.

We examined one another in the moonlight. How he had aged! How shrunken had he become! Even then I was not certain why I had come to him. Though something in me shifted when I saw that he smiled at the sight of me.

"I…" he began, then faltered, then looked at me again with something like pride in his eyes. "I have changed."

These three words hung heavy between us.

"Then you must prove it," I said.

"I will." He was eager. "Give me the opportunity and I will prove it to you."

"You understand that I could kill you?" I said simply. "I ought to have done it before."

Frankenstein held up his hand, a finger extended. "One chance," he said. "That's all I ask."

From somewhere deeper in the asylum, I heard the sounds of footsteps and voices. I stepped closer to the bars, saw the pitiful frame of the old man beyond.

"I will set you free," I said, "and I will give you seven years of liberty. But in that time you must work only good. Do you understand me, my father-mother? Only good."

And at this, the wretch nodded his head and somehow (I cannot say why given all that had passed between us) somehow I believed him.

My exile had taught me pity. I only hope that it did not teach me undue credulity also.

The following night there was an incident at the asylum.

One of the doors was broken, one of the cells destroyed and one of the inmates escaped.

I will not set down here who was responsible, though I have little doubt that you can guess.

And so I loosed him again upon the world. You may judge me for this, my friend, and I would not blame you. Those seven years have gone now and I am in search of him once more.

Will you pray for me, my friend?

There is difficult work ahead and I will have need of strength and courage. Bless you, sir, and thank you once more. A final meeting awaits and so I must away.

May your own Creator bless you and keep you.

A Friend

PART SIX

A LETTER FROM THE REVEREND C. W. LEIGH-STANLEY TO JESSE MALONE

24TH AUGUST, 1850
THE VICARAGE, CRISPIN RYE

My dear Mr Malone,

I dare say that you were not expecting to receive this letter. Indeed, I ought by rights to begin with a complete apology for leaving you and Mr Hubert Crowe with such rude alacrity upon our last encounter.

No, rather I should be more honest with you even than that. Please, sir, accept my apologies for *fleeing* from the very sight of you both.

It is, I am sure, rather cold comfort now but it was not merely from the view of you and Mr Crowe that I ran but from London herself. I write these words back in the relative (though, I fear, only temporary) safety of Crispin Rye. I thought that I might be able to face poor Greene again, after all that had happened, but I found sadly that I could not.

Perhaps had you two gentlemen not been there? Had Mr Crowe not sported that strange, wild gleam in his eye which spoke of some incipient obsession? Yes, then, perhaps the moment may have passed differently. Yet such is the power of coincidence or, at least, what passes for coincidence in an earthly realm which, I still have to believe, possesses some ineffable order which we mortals are not permitted to see in its entirety.

Now, my former friend and neighbour, Mr Greene, is due to be hanged, very soon now, and I am, at least in part, to blame for his fate.

If you are the sort of fellow whom I take you to be,

I imagine that you will now be desirous of an explanation, however partial, of my own role in this tragedy. This, at least if you will indulge me for a while, I shall now endeavour to provide. This letter of mine will have to be a long one and it will cause me great pain to write it, not only pain of the figurative kind but of the literal as my hand aches abominably since an incident which took two of my fingers on my left hand. Yet I must go on.

I heard a little of what the condemned man was telling you before I could bring myself to enter the cell. Evidently, he had been speaking for some hours and had told you a good deal that was preliminary to the tragedy. Yet there is much that came after which you have still to learn.

Much!

―――

I have, as you know, acted for many years as the parish priest for Crispin Rye. It is a small place, sparsely populated, and my duties have often been far from taxing. There were even times as a very much younger man when I wondered why I had been given so calm and undemanding a set of duties and when I wondered also whether this period might not represent only the first act of some greater story, that the Lord had placed me there in order to play a larger role in His struggle. It was during the spring of 1843 that this call to arms finally arrived.

When the writer Nathaniel Greene and his wife, Alice, had first appeared in the district some three years prior, their coming had attracted much interest and excitement in the neighbourhood. These sentiments soon faded when it became plain that the pair had about them not the merest shred of glamour or intrigue, and that they meant to keep themselves private to a point which stopped short only barely of outright reclusiveness.

There was, I believe, talk of children, with which they were not to be blessed, and of some urgent work by Mr Greene himself (a survey of the secret folklore of the metropolis, which never saw print and which never shall do now). And so soon enough the interest of the locals shifted towards other, readier sources of gossip and really very little was remarked of concerning the couple, save that Mrs Greene was seen occasionally about the village, looking resentful and uninterested, and that Mr Greene was rumoured, in rather a regrettable manner, to pursue a number of dalliances in a variety of towns and villages beside the sea.

Nonetheless, I took a particular interest in them from the start (educated men not being common in that part of the world) and struck up, if not quite a friendship then at least an amicable acquaintanceship with the writer. Aside from his association with that disreputable figure from Nevisham Row known as "the Judge", we got along well enough and would meet occasionally for conversations of an agreeable kind.

It was in January of 1843, however, when matters began to change.

Rumours began to emanate from that isolated house. One or other of his drunken servants hinted darkly, while in thrall to strong drink, of a new visitor there and of certain horrible designs of his. There was talk of building work being done and of odd devices being constructed.

The so-called "Judge" was said to have intervened, only to disappear soon afterwards.

Around the same time there were, I regret to say, some outrages committed in my own graveyard — coffins disturbed and even a pair of newly laid bodies dismembered. It was not until the night of the March storm that I was able to piece at least a little of the truth together. I know that Greene has already told you something of our meeting on the eighth of that month, an occasion on which he was able to furnish me with one crucial fact to which I had yet to be privy — the name of their visitor.

The storm of the eighth was a villainous one and, having been shown by my sexton, Mr Cassell, the scene of the latest outrage in the earth (a body disturbed) I retired to bed.

I locked my doors and prayed. I listened to the thunder and the lightning. I knew nothing of what was occurring at the Hall. Even if I had done so, I could have done nothing to stop it. I hope, Mr Malone, that you believe me in this.

It is often difficult, is it not, when recollecting an evening of great significance, only subsequently realised, to place a retrospective emphasis on some stray detail or other? It may be so in this case, I cannot say. Yet I remain certain that I fell into an uneasy slumber on the night of the storm only to be awakened shortly after midnight by a mighty peal of thunder and a dreadful crack of lightning.

This, as you were told, was the very moment of filthy creation. Though I could not then have understood why, I awoke in an agony of fearful expectation. My skin prickled and my heart pounded wildly.

Although I had a memory of dreaming it seemed to me that I had waked from the worst nightmare of my life and that, in the words of the third chapter of the book of Job: "the thing which I greatly feared is come upon me, and that which I was afraid of is come unto me".

I sat up in bed and lit a candle. I listened awhile to the storm but, its energies now seemingly spent, it began first to dissipate and then to move away. I prayed, a habit about which I fear, I am not always as assiduous as I might be, until, at last, some measure of solace was returned to me. I was able, if fitfully, to return to sleep.

In the morning, things seemed a little better and more settled and that feeling of dread which had crept over me like a thick fog in the night seemed to have lifted.

The rest of the week seemed to continue in this vein. The weather improved (always heartening) and there were no further storms. I also dared to hope that the outrages in our cemetery had ceased as days went by without incident or upset of any kind.

It was in general as though a shadow which had crept unseen over Crispin Rye had begun to recede, leaving every one of us blinking and confused, but relieved, in the sunshine.

During this period I had much to occupy me, the aftermath of the disinterments being considerable, and it was not until the Friday morning of that week that I was able at last to pay a visit to the Hall.

Our discussion in The Deacon's Resort (interrupted as it had been by the sexton) had been weighing heavily upon my mind. It was with some trepidation, that I made the approach on that bright morning, walking the long pathway which led to the Hall, only to find it wearing an unfamiliar aspect – one of near-absolute desertion.

It had ever been an eerie place, of course, shunned by the

villagers and by the residents of the neighbouring hamlets for a number of foolish and superstitious reasons. It was no accident that Fieldwick Hall had long been untenanted before the arrival of the Greenes, nor that they could find no other servants willing to reside there save for Mr and Mrs Tebb. Yet I had never seen it in quite such a state of absence and dereliction as I did that morning.

As you have discovered, it has grown considerably worse since then.

There were no signs of life. I rang the bell and waited. No answer came. I knocked on the door, louder and with greater intensity that I might otherwise have done. Still, there was nothing. I tried the door and found it open. I pushed my way inside. The interior was dark and there was within a scent of stale wood smoke and charring.

I called out into the gloom. "Mr Greene!"

Nothing stirred.

"Nathaniel!"

I hesitated. I was about to call out once again and then I heard what sounded to me like two sets of footsteps, one confident and firm, the other more uncertain and even somehow shambling.

I turned around and saw that a pair of shapes had emerged from what I believed to be the pantry.

One was the familiar figure of Greene himself. The other, much shorter and slighter, stood a little behind him and was wreathed in shadow.

"Reverend?"

Mr Greene's voice had a distant quality, as though he was still groggy from a lingering illness, or from the consequences of some wild debauch the preceding night.

"What are you doing here?" he asked.

I explained. "I was concerned after our conversation in The Deacon's Resort, I came to see you as quickly as I could…"

I looked all around me, searching for some indication as to how this state of things had come to pass. The person who stood behind my friend and neighbour did not move.

"Has something happened here?" I asked, perhaps with some redundancy.

"Much…" Greene said softly. "Much has happened here."

"Your servants…" I began.

"Gone," said Greene and there crept now into his voice a shade more animation. "Fled. Both of them. Along with the visitor and… my wife."

"Why?" I asked. "My dear fellow, why?"

Greene barked a short, hard laugh. "They found they could not look upon their handiwork. My wife's dream was given to her and she shunned it. But where they saw horror I saw only love."

The figure behind him shuffled from foot to foot.

"Nathaniel, if all the household has fled then who is it that stands behind you in the gloom?"

"This," said Nathaniel Greene very calmly, "is my son. Say hello now, my darling, to the reverend."

The shape behind him lurched forwards on command and stepped into the light. At the sight of him, its tongue seemed caught in my throat. Words died on my lips. He was as nothing I had seen before.

It was a boy – not more than six or seven years of age – but not like any boy whom I had ever met.

His face was a grotesque patchwork of skin and scars, stitched unevenly together. His hair was but a ragged clump. His hands were twisted and deformed, his feet misshapen clods.

His eyes were a terrible shade of yellow. He peered out at me beseechingly from a body that looked born of wickedness and pain.

"Hell-o..." he said. As he spoke, I heard that his voice was a dreadful grinding thing, like a spade hitting flint in the frozen ground.

"Nathaniel..." I started. "Who... how...?"

"I told you." Greene looked as though he had never been more certain of a thing in all his life. "This is my son. His name is Adam."

After the initial jolt of horror had passed I was able to master myself and offer Mr Greene a firm, unwavering smile. "I imagine," I said, "that there is something of a tale attached to this new arrival?"

At this, the boy gurgled, a painful sound which I assumed, entirely erroneously, betokened his proximity to idiocy.

"He's laughing," Greene said softly. "But as to your question, Reverend, you are quite correct. Shall we three take tea together? And then I can explain as best I can."

And so we sat down together in the sparse and peeling drawing room of the Hall. Greene himself made us a pot of tea and produced from somewhere a small tin of cake which the boy seized with all the vulgar avidity of a starving chimpanzee. When I remember the conversation that was had then between Mr Greene and I, it is in my imagination forever punctuated by the sound of desperate and inexpert mastication which emanated from the boy.

The content of our discussion you will by now already know. Greene gave me a brisk, unsentimental outline of what had occurred, of the malfeasance of his wife and the Genevese physician, of the fate of the draper's widow and of the dark miracle in the nighttime.

"This is fantastic," I said, once he had finished. "Incredible. I would once have said impossible. And I still say – *blasphemous*."

This was the response that the moment seemed to expect of me. I was not certain that I believed the words even as I spoke them.

"Reverend," said Greene, "just look at the evidence of your eyes."

We gazed together at the hunched, simian figure of the child as he smeared cake crumbs into his misshapen fingers before licking clean the residue.

"So what will you do?" I asked.

"Just what I must." He spoke as though there was no question as to how he should act. "Look after that boy. Raise him. Teach him. Guide him."

"But... surely. My God! He's not natural. How do you know he will even grow... mature... like a real boy?"

"He is real," Greene said simply. "For he is mine, I knew it. The moment that I saw him I knew that he was mine. Love, Reverend! Love such as I have never known before and in such bountiful quantity!"

I looked into his eyes and I saw there a solemnity of purpose which struck me as obscurely terrible. I saw that everything he said he believed wholeheartedly and without question, and

I think I saw also something of those dreadful extremities to which his newfound responsibilities would lead him.

Greene leaned forwards and placed a hand upon mine. "Will you help me?" he asked. "To keep this boy safe?"

The child began to whoop and watch the path of some languid fly in the air.

"There may be those," Greene went on, "who do not understand him as I do." He must have seen the hesitation in my face for he all but gripped my hand now with a pressure that spoke of desperation. "Please."

So, what else could I do, Mr Malone, but offer the man my pledge?

Soon afterwards, I bade farewell and left, troubled, of course, in my heart, but feeling also that I had at last been granted by the Lord that purpose for which I had been set down in the first place in Crispin Rye.

There is no time now to tell you all that transpired, Mr Malone, in the seven years that followed, years in which I did all that I could to help Mr Greene and his strange, ill-formed progeny, years in which – though we did not know it – the clock was ticking ever downwards to catastrophe.

Although their situation degenerated into something not far from penury, Greene seemed somehow able to provide for the boy, keeping him safe, fed and well cared for. I assisted where I could and I did a great deal to dissuade curious eyes from looking too deeply in the direction of the edge of our village.

Thankfully, we had few visitors and the inhabitants were,

at first, easy enough to distract from what was in their midst. That Mr and Mrs Tebb had disappeared with the lady and the stranger was helpful to our cause for they were no longer present to spread either rumour or vitriol. There were some difficult questions from parishioners, of course, though I batted them away with vague talk of a hitherto unmentioned nephew arriving unexpectedly at the Hall.

Greene played his own part, by sinking into a state close to that of the recluse, to the degree that he was thought of in the village less and less often.

For a long while, I was his only guest, often bearing gifts of food or books. He had begun to educate the little creature in his care who (in spite of outward appearances) grew to have a surprisingly lively mind, with an especial facility for the classics and for the Gospels.

There was for a time in that place, Mr Malone, much kindness and affection, for all that certain undercurrents were already visible.

I believe that I can demonstrate this growing shadow, and show you how Mr Greene went from solitary father to condemned man by way of several separate episodes, each an escalation from the next. And in doing so, I can give you just a flavour, Mr Malone, of the dreamlike strangeness of that seven-year span.

The first such incident took place not more than six months after the appearance of the boy, Adam, in the September of 1843, and occurred during a very early lesson in which I was endeavouring to educate the creature.

His was ever a mind predisposed to the asking of questions and he was always presenting me with a torrent of them. Greene had fashioned a rudimentary schoolroom in one of the outbuildings by the exterior of the Hall itself. You passed it, Mr Malone, but I did not draw attention to it, for the place has for me rather a mingled set of memories. At the time, however, it was well sufficient for our purposes. I brought many books from my own library. There was chalk and there was a blackboard.

As to how I had come to play tutor the boy? It was, of course, in part at the pleading of Nathaniel but it was also in consequence of prayer. In the quiet and sober darkness of our little church, I had asked the Lord for guidance and His response had been quite clear and without the merest shred of ambiguity.

This was the moment, this the task and I was to be the instrument of His will. I wonder now at the nature of that soft, still voice which spoke to me in that sepulchred gloom, even at its true identity. Though I fear that to do so for too long will lead me down a path of unhappiness which can culminate only in despair and madness.

To return to the nub of the matter. I agreed to tutor the boy as best I could and to instil in him not only his numbers, letters, a little Greek and Latin but also a firm and imperishable love of, and adherence to, the teachings of Christ. The little Creature's arrival into the world was by no means ordinary and I knew that he had to be filled up, as soon as we could contrive it, with all the teachings, maxims and morals as would befit a human child. What began as duty, however, grew into pleasure.

I came soon enough to look forward to our thrice-weekly discussions. Nathaniel spent much time with the boy himself and proved to be a tender and comprehensive tutor. Between the two of us, I doubt that there can have been a boy in the country who was educated in so short a space of time and with such verve, save, perhaps, for certain first sons of the nobility.

It is only a small thing, this memory, an inkling of what was to follow and it took the form of a single, uncomfortable question of a kind with which many owners of children will surely be familiar. I was in the midst of a discussion of certain of the Pauline epistles when the boy raised his hand, a regular enough incident at that time.

"Yes, Adam," I said.

"I have a question."

Now, to any from the outside, the child's voice would still have sounded a rough, unnatural thing though I had, by then, become accustomed to it.

"Then you must ask it," I said, perhaps a little wearily.

"Whence do children come?"

"From love," I said quickly, all at once, and without hesitation. "From the love of a man and a woman as was ordained by God."

"Are they born?"

"Yes, Adam," I said. "Of course they are."

"And made in an act of darkness?"

"If you like," I said, rather uncertainly, while wondering to myself where he might have encountered such a phrase.

"But not, I think, Reverend… not me?"

"My boy," I said gently. "Whatever do you mean by that?"

He sighed and he slumped forwards on his little wooden desk. I stepped towards him and saw that there were glistening tears at the edges of his yellow eyes. His tears were not clear and altogether colourless – as are those of God's own creations – but rather a dirty brown hue, like rainwater which has sat too long upon the ground. I realised then that I did not know quite what Nathaniel had told the child of his own origins.

"You were made in another way," I said. "You are quite unique. There is nobody else like you in all the wide world. But you are watched over, my boy, and you are loved – truly loved – by two fathers, one earthly and one divine."

The boy drew in a breath and wiped away his tears. He looked at me pugnaciously. "I think you are wrong," he said.

"I promise you," I protested. "You are loved."

"I know that," said the child as though it were a self-evident truth. "I didn't mean it quite that way."

"What then?" I asked.

"I am not the first. I am not the only one. There is another. I have a brother. For I have seen him." He tapped the side of his head. "And he is coming for me."

I could think of nothing whatever to say to this. And there was a very long silence indeed in that schoolroom before we commenced the lesson once again.

Two years later. 1845. It was not long since Christmastime, always a busy stretch of days for me, in that period before the new year in which Mary had rested with her newborn and before the arrival of the Magi.

I was alone in my church, performing some necessary custodial duties and enjoying the peaceful stillness of the place. We have an especially beautiful piece of stained glass, Mr Malone, which depicts the creation of Eve from the rib-bone of her husband. I shall miss it when I leave as I will miss much (though by no means all) about this little place. It was upon this scene that I was gazing, in a momentary respite from my labours when I heard the sound of the door being opened and then of hurried footsteps.

I called out. "Who's there?"

The voice that answered was familiar to me. "Sorry... sorry, Reverend..."

I turned to acknowledge the arrival. "You need never apologise," I said, "for entering a house of God."

The man nodded gratefully. "Obliged to you."

His name was Barrendale and there is one of his sort in every English village. Born to slipshod parents, he was a petty criminal or at least a man who sailed often close to the edges of the law. Not yet thirty, he looked a good decade older, red-faced and balding, a walking testament to poor living and to too great an acquaintance with sin.

He was, for all of that, a good-hearted fellow, who might well have been a finer man had only his start in his life been a kinder one.

"Whatever is the matter, Mr Barrendale?" I asked. "You look to me to be in a state of some considerable distress."

I saw then that he was out of breath, and I wondered if he had been running to reach the church.

"Sit down," I said and he seated himself at the end of a pew. "Tell me what ails you."

He seemed to collect himself. "Saw something," he said. "Something bad."

"Where?" I asked, though in truth I already suspected the answer.

"At the Hall."

"Whatever were you doing there?" I asked (though, once again, I had my suspicions).

"Just walking," he said, sounding both implausible and plaintive. "Just taking the air, Reverend."

"It is a little late for a stroll, surely?"

Barrendale shot me a truculent look. "Walking," he said again.

"You know," I said softly, "that poaching is a crime which is taken very seriously nowadays by the courts?"

"No, Reverend, no. I wouldn't know anything about that."

Of course, I just let the matter lie, being doubtful, in any case, that Nathaniel would ever notice were his grounds to be filled up with local poachers, so engrossed had he become in his life with the boy. "What happened?"

Barrendale seemed by now to have mastered himself a little more. "There is something wrong," he said. "Oh, but there is something so badly wrong with that place."

"Many before you have said so. There have always been rumours and stories. Old wives' tales, most of them. But what did you see?"

"A boy," he said. "Yes, a boy of a sort – but I don't think he's a natural one."

"You saw a boy at the Hall? Why, surely," I said as carefully as I could, "surely that is only Mr Greene's nephew?"

Barrendale scowled. "Is that what they're calling him?"

"That is what he is."

Our poacher shook his head. "Not natural," he said again. "Made up of shreds and patches. And I saw him dancing, Reverend... in the moonlight. Naked to the waist, sir, and dancing by the Hall. Like some wild puppet. It's not natural, sir. It's not right."

"Oh, but he is an unusual child, I believe. Yes, to be sure. But there is nothing in the least bit sinister to it."

Barrendale shook his head. "Old Greene knows all about him. I watched, Reverend. I hid and I watched and I saw him call the boy in."

"Well then. That all seems unremarkable enough to me. An uncle and his nephew. Nothing more than that."

"'Tis the house, sir. The house. It calls evil to its bosom. That place needs burning, sir. Burning to the ground."

"Let us not commit further evil in the name of conquering it," I said firmly. "Now, perhaps, it would be best if you simply kept away from Fieldwick Hall henceforth."

Barrendale nodded again though he seemed far from certain as to my suggestion.

"Shall we pray together?" I asked and, somewhat to my relief, the man agreed.

As we prayed I could not help but notice how much more fervent Barrendale seemed than ever he had before and I reflected, perhaps unwisely or unfairly, that a moderate portion of fear seemed to have had upon him a most medicinal effect.

In the morning I went to the Hall, hurrying there discreetly not long after dawn when there were fewer watchful eyes abroad.

I found Nathaniel alone in the library looking out towards the line of trees from which the madman, Frankenstein, once had stumbled. It occurred to me again how vulnerable he was here, alone in that great house, without servants of any kind and with only the boy for company.

He would be easy prey for any determined bandit or brigand. In this I was, to a large degree, mistaken, as you shall shortly see.

On that morning, Greene was in pensive mood, even a little dazed in his manner. It was not in many ways, you understand, a healthy life that he lived at that time.

"What's happened?" he said without any words of greeting or introduction, and without wrenching his gaze from the patch of wood beyond.

"Nathaniel," I said, "you need to be more careful about the boy."

"He's been seen?"

With brisk urgency, I gave him Barrendale's account.

Mr Greene seemed unconcerned. "No harm," he said. "No harm done there."

"People are talking," I said. "They are afraid. These are ideal circumstances for... unrest."

Greene turned now to face me. "It's the house," he said. "The house will keep them away, at least for now. Fieldwick Hall... both beckons and repels." He waved his left hand vaguely through the air. "This place... has many moods."

As if in response to this remark, there came from overhead a terrific crash followed by a hoarse cry and the sound of a door being slammed so hard as to all but shatter its hinges. A flicker of strong emotion passed too quickly across the face of Mr Greene.

"He is... struggling," he said. "This season has proved difficult to him."

"The boy sounds angry," I ventured.

"I think he is." Greene seemed numb and the thought

occurred to me that he may have already taken a drink that day. Another howl echoed down from a higher level, then silence. "You should go," said Greene. "Schooling will resume in the new year. He will have calmed himself by then." I did not move. "Thank you for bringing me the news about the poacher, Reverend." His tone now grew formal. "I shall be more careful in the days to come. But you may leave now. I am sure that you must have plentiful demands upon your time."

Understanding that I was being dismissed, I said goodbye and left Greene to his library and his thoughts, but I did not leave the Hall. Instead, I trod lightly up the staircase in search of the boy. The rooms here were in large part abandoned and left to moulder. I tried four chambers, each thick with dust and cobwebs, before I discovered young Adam, lying half-sprawled upon the filthy floor, his back against the wall.

"My boy?" I said.

He looked up and I saw sour resentment in his pale yellow eyes. "Why are you here?" he asked.

"I heard of your distress."

At this, he turned his gaze away from me.

"What is it, my boy?" I asked. "What ails you?"

Perhaps, Mr Malone, you will consider the stratagem of mine to be too meek a thing; perhaps you would have thought the application of the rod to have been a better solution to the Creature's rough conduct. Many, I dare say, would agree with you though I make no apology for taking a gentler tack.

I knelt beside him and took his hands in mine.

"My boy…"

He would not meet my eyes but he spoke again, his strange voice sounding still more jagged than usual.

"The nature of it..." he said. "That is, the nature of my birth. It has d——d me from the first."

"No," I said. "No, that cannot be true. I refute it. My faith refutes it. We are all of us born with a degree of sin, but we all stand also bathed in the love of the Lamb. Whatever abnormal means brought about the moment of your birth are as nothing in the eyes of God. For you and your life and all that you will yet achieve are part of the Lord's design. Even your creator, that wicked man, even he is part of God's plan."

When he looked upon me then there was hope in his eyes. Wordlessly, he too got upon his knees and, just as I had done the night before in the company of Mr Barrendale, I led us both in prayer.

Yet even as I spoke the words of homage and petition, I felt move within the recesses of my mind a dreadful shudder of doubt.

Almost three years later. The autumn of 1848. Past eleven at night.

I had intended to work late but had become engrossed in the current edition of *Household Words* and I was seated by the vicarage fire, when I heard upon my door a timid knock – a scratch more than anything else. It was a plaintive scraping which seemed to speak of exhaustion and desperation. I fear that I was not best pleased at the sound for I was enjoying, perhaps selfishly, the long evening's recreation and I have done much over the years to discourage the unplanned appearance upon my threshold of parishioners at all hours of day and night (so often a bane of the country parson's existence).

With a single "tut" of irritation, I rose to my feet and strode to the door. Peering out into the gloom, I had to look down to discover the source of the noise. It was the boy – the Greene boy, of course – who was looking up at me with his yellow eyes.

He seemed still more pale than was usual. He trembled. And there was, I saw, blood upon his fingers and caked also into his nails.

"Whatever has happened?" I asked and I realised as I did so that I had long been expecting to speak such words to that child at such an hour and in sight of blood. He said nothing but only crooked a lumpen finger and beckoned.

I stepped closer and I saw that he had been crying.

He made a noise which sounded like a metallic wrenching. "Please."

He beckoned again and, without questioning the urgency of the moment, I stepped out to follow him into the night.

Adam was fleeter of foot than his lumpen form might suggest and I had to increase my pace to match his. The vicarage is at the heart of the village yet we passed no other person as we walked, under the moon, northwards in the direction of Fieldwick Hall. This did not surprise me.

"What is it?" I asked again. "What's wrong?"

The child did not reply and only hurried onwards. Out of the village we went and down into the fields beyond. The Hall loomed ahead of us and I assumed it was to be our destination. Yet the boy did not slow but lurched on towards the line of trees.

"This way," he said. "Be quick now. Swift."

We went together under the canopy of branches. Strange

how noisy are woodlands at night, the creaks and the scuffles, the snaps and little movements, the sighing of the cold wind through dead leaves.

I felt at once a spasm of unaccountable fear which I had never felt in the presence of the boy since our first meeting.

"You need to explain to me," I began and was about to add the phrase "precisely what it is that is happening here" when I heard a fresh sound in the distance, a frail yet recognisable voice.

"Leigh-Stanley? Is that you, man?"

At this, the boy grew animated. "Father!" The word was an urgent moan. He beckoned me on and his meaning was quite clear: hurry, hurry, we have to help him.

"I'm here!" I called out, my own voice a puny thing in that forest.

The boy beckoned and went on and so I followed. Our boots cracked over windfall and our approach scattered all the little beasts and creatures who lived there. The light of the moon was dim and often obscured by cloud. I pressed on regardless.

At last, we found him, Nathaniel Greene, lying on a rough bed of bracken. He was bleeding from a cut in his forehead and I saw that his leg was at a terrible angle. His face shone with perspiration.

"Thank God," he said at the sight of us.

"Him first," I said. "And after that you should thank your boy for it was he who fetched me and brought me here."

Greene gave the child who stood then by my side, a furtive, understanding glance. Then he shook his head towards me in a tight, grim motion.

"Oh," I said. "I see."

I went to him and I lifted him up and together the three of us walked very slowly back towards the Hall.

Mr Greene's injuries were severe – a gash to his head which left a slight scar and a broken left leg which never entirely healed. There were also some very curious wounds inflicted on his hands and fingers, and, in particular, the knuckles of both hands, some of them like bite-marks and suggestive of worse besides.

Greene would never tell me quite how it had happened or of the nature of that quarrel which, I presumed, had led to that ghastly affray. All that he ever said by way of explanation was this, delivered the following day, after a visit made by a baffled and suspicious physician from Taverham: "it's the most overwhelming kind of love," he said. "The most unexpected and overwhelming kind of love. There is nothing whatever that boy could do or say which would remove so much as a splinter of it. It's love born of blood, you see, stronger than any other sort. Do you understand?"

I said that being a childless man, I could not.

"Quite so," he replied. "Quite so."

And I saw to my surprise that he was smiling.

I am endeavouring to provide to you a kind of survey of how it was in those days, and of the many different aspects of the complicated relationship between Adam and Nathaniel Greene. Their life together at the Hall always contained within it the seeds of that eventual tragedy which arrived earlier this year, though much was to befall them until that solemn date.

In the spring of 1849, there was a curious incident which I had half-foreseen when I had visited Nathaniel after Christmas almost four years before.

I never knew the full details of the matter, but the essential facts are these: on the night of April 22nd a gang of four men broke into Fieldwick Hall with — by their own subsequent admission — the express purpose of robbing the owner. They were not local men but came from somewhere near the coast, up towards Lowestoft. Quite how they heard of the circumstances of Mr Greene is not known, though I expect that gossip and rumour travel at least as quickly through the criminal fraternity as they do through any other. In whatever fashion, this quartet of criminals had heard that Fieldwick Hall lay open and undefeated.

The ringleader — one Silas Guthrie — said later in court, by which time he was by all accounts a shadow of his former self, that the gang only went to "see what was there for the taking" and to "do no harm to the owner seeing as he was a rich one who had no need of so much."

By this, I understand Mr Guthrie to have meant that this place seemed like easy prey and that its eccentric owner would present no serious challenge. In the making of these assumptions, these gentlemen committed the worst mistake of their lives.

They broke into the Hall not long after midnight. Nathaniel Greene was asleep but the child was not. They discovered him, according to Guthrie, in the library and tried to overpower him. It was then that the difficulties of these men began in earnest. Guthrie would not say much more except to confirm that they were chased from the Hall. He would not ever say by whom, though the implication was clear.

Guthrie himself seemed to find an odd kind of comfort, first in pleading guilty and then in the length of his incarceration.

Of his three co-conspirators, one went missing on the morning after the attempted theft. Another was committed to an asylum rather than stand trial. The third accepted his sentence without ever speaking a word, not even to account for those dreadful lacerations and marks upon his legs and arms. It has even been said – though this is surely nothing more than a piece of fanciful embroidery – that not a single word has passed his lips ever since and that he spends his days now as a mute.

The trial might have caused a sensation but in some fashion it was kept quiet and passed quickly and without further incident.

Neither Nathaniel or the boy would ever tell me the truth about the events of that night, save for just one thing. Half asleep once, young Adam murmured to me: "I did only what my brother would have done."

The phrase was situated in no particular context at all yet I have drawn my own conclusions about its significance. No doubt you, Mr Malone, will do the same.

Time grows short and we should get to the finish of it. One more incident – suggestive and quietly dreadful – and then I must face the final tragedy.

In the third week of January of this very year, I took myself away from the parish for a long weekend's stay in the seaside town of Cromer at the invitation of the mother of an old schoolfriend of mine, now, sadly deceased.

The lady, though a gracious host, was advanced in years and

inclined to sleepiness. There was little enough for us to discuss once the topics first of her much-lamented son and then of her own fears for the hereafter had been, at least temporarily, exhausted.

And so I took up the habit, while I was her guest, to taking two long walks a day – one not long after we had breakfasted, the other in the afternoon, an hour or two before the sun was due to set. It was an arrangement which suited us both very well for we were by nature solitary creatures. I enjoyed the quiet of the beach but also, paradoxically, the sound of it, of stones underfoot and of the roaring of the waves.

It was on the last walk of my final day with the lady, as I stepped along the little strip of pebbled land with the town upon my left and the great grey surging bank of the sea to my right, when I saw an approaching figure whom I recognised at once, though the realisation was not pleasant to me. He doubtless felt the same. Yet the beach was empty save for the two of us and there was no visible means of extricating ourselves from the encounter without grave discourtesy. We had no choice but to hail one another.

"Reverend!" He was a big man, clad in black, who had grown still more corpulent since we had last met.

"Judge," I said, once we stood opposite one another. I gave the man the compliment of using his old title, although I fear that my voice was not altogether free of the sardonic. "What an unexpected pleasure it is to see you." As a rural clergyman, one soon becomes accomplished at delivering the insincere with conviction.

"What brings you here?" he asked.

I told him my reasons before asking the same of him.

Both of us eyed the way ahead, hoping that we might soon be on our way.

"Why, I live up here now," he said. "Well... not far. My old bones ached to see the sea, I think. I believe it's in my blood."

As far as I knew, the old fraud possessed not the slightest maritime connection. Yet I murmured an emollient "of course" just the same.

"So..." I felt that the gentleman wished to leave our conversation there and I was most certainly happy to collude with him in this — yet there was some part of him which, it seemed, could not resist another question. "Is all quite well?" he asked. "In the village of Crispin Rye?"

He spoke these words with the implicit conviction that things were very far indeed from being "all well" in Crispin Rye and that he was in possession of fairly robust intelligence which would shortly prove the contrary.

"Well enough," I lied.

The Judge winced.

"You have heard otherwise?" I include a question mark here for the purposes of good grammar though I don't believe that it was audible in my words upon that beach.

"I may..." The Judge looked unsettled. "I may have heard one or two things. Rumours. Gossip, I suppose."

I said nothing but only gazed levelly at him. Beside us, the sea roared and seethed and hissed. Suddenly in motion, he leaned forwards and seized my arm. "It's that house, isn't it? It's the Hall? That d—d bl—y house."

"I am not certain," I said, for, even now, I cannot quite bring myself to credit every one of the wild suppositions about Fieldwick Hall, though of course I have my suspicions. "But any state of affairs which exist in that house are, I assure you, both well-observed and safe enough."

Gulls shrieked overhead, sounding, in the circumstances, too close to laughter.

The Judge shook his head. "That d—d fool Greene should have listened to me years ago. Should never have bought the place. You'd better warn him, Reverend."

"Warn him of what?"

"You can tell him from me what he's up to in that place... that *thing* which lives with him... It's not gone unnoticed. And unless he gets it under control very soon now... well, steps will have to be taken. Do you understand me? Steps will have to be taken."

This small speech done, he exhaled, nodded once and strode away. I did not speak or seek to stop him, grateful for his leaving and for the soothing sound of the waves.

I had no particular wish to continue my walk after this disagreeable encounter. To turn around then, however, and to start back towards the town would be to run the risk of catching up with the Judge for I am a fast walker and he, as I have said, seemed increasingly weighed down by corpulence. In consequence, I idled a while longer until the fellow was entirely out of sight and all that I could see was sky and sea, rocky beach and dark ocean. As I strolled uneasily, I wondered at the Judge's warnings and I almost, if not quite, succeeded in dismissing his threats as so much unfounded bluster.

At length, having decided that sufficient time had elapsed, I turned upon my heel and started back in the direction of the town.

Then something (who can say quite what?) made me look

over my shoulder one final time. I had assumed that the beach was deserted. I saw now that it was not.

A man stood in the distance, watching me. Twilight had by then begun to fall and I could not make out his features but he was tall, so very tall, taller than any mortal man has any right to be. As if at the sight of me, he raised his great left hand in some obscure gesture, whether of warning or of invitation I could not be sure.

I peered closer, though I dared not move and seemed to see that he was in some fashion a patchwork thing, and that he possessed some awful familiarity. I could not help but scream. My own hands I flung up towards my eyes. When I lowered them again, the watcher was gone.

It was at a brisk pace indeed that I hurried back after that to the mother of my old friend. I no longer checked my speed for fear of seeing the Judge again for I felt a cold certainty that something of true fate and consequence trod now upon my heels.

After this, the crisis came swiftly indeed.

I had not been home in Crispin Rye for more than a week after my sojourn at the coast before a tap came on Saturday afternoon at the vicarage door.

Even the most tactless of my parishioners know that this is not a span of hours in which to trouble me lightly for I am then generally to be discovered in the composition of my weekly sermon.

It was in no good humour, then, that I rose from the desk in my study and hurried to the door so that I might chase the caller courteously away. When I opened up, however, it was to see that there was not one visitor but two.

Both were known to me, the first directly and the second by dreadful reputation.

Mrs Alice Greene stood before me. It had been seven years since I had seen her last and time had been kind to her indeed, so kind in fact that it seemed possible that she looked younger than on our last meeting. Certainly, she seemed well-groomed and also to possess the distinct air of money. Her dress looked new and her hair seemed more lustrous than before.

"Reverend," she smiled. "I am so sorry to interrupt you when you are in the midst of preparing your homily. But I was passing by and I simply had to introduce you to a very good friend of mine." She indicated the elderly and visibly frail personage who stood a few paces behind her – and he who represented the reason, I had no doubt, for her apparent rejuvenation.

"This," she said, "is Victor—"

I interrupted: "I know, madam, who he is.*"

He was smaller than I had expected, slighter in build and crooked now with age. Still there was no mistaking the terrible force of his character. Why, he seemed almost to burn with it, with the dreadful spirit of unfettered blasphemy.

---

* Before he died, my father said to me that he had carried out researches as to what the lady and the gentleman might have gotten up to in these seven long years away from the village. He said there wasn't much to be found and that there was nothing he could ever prove but he was very interested in the doings of a "Dr and Mrs Smythe" who were at this time active in the north of Britain, based in the city of York and often to be found touring its provinces selling all manner of quack cures and remedies. The rise in the same period of despoiled graveyards and cemeteries in that part of the world is perhaps nothing to be wondered at.

"I somehow never thought that you would arrive so quietly," I said to the creator of monsters. "Nor knock upon my door with such soft deference."

Victor Frankenstein smiled a careful smile. "There are many misconceptions about me, Reverend," he said, and I heard in his voice a flavour of the continent. "And if you were to invite us in, my dear fellow, perhaps you will permit me to set the worst of them aright."

I thought of old stories then, of boggarts and witches and creatures who suckle upon blood. Was there not something in the annals of folklore about their needing to be invited into one's home? A sour irony, of course, that Nathaniel was the man who would surely know the answer to that.

"What do you want?" I asked and I became aware as I did so that I was gripping tightly onto my own doorframe.

Mrs Greene said: "We have a small favour to ask of you. Nothing substantial. And nothing which, as a man of God, will go against your calling. On the contrary, if you do as we ask, you will rather be acting for the right party in your long crusade."

I frowned at the odd formulation of her words. There was a nervousness to her, I thought, a deep-set sense of anxiety beneath her cool exterior. I looked at them both, this transformed woman and the architect of what I knew to be an assault against the very laws of creation.

"You had better come in," I said and, Lord save me, I ushered them both inside.

I settled Frankenstein and Mrs Greene in the parlour while I made us all a pot of tea then bore it through upon a platter.

I do not know why but for a second I was reminded of the severed head of John the Baptist being brought to Herod upon a different kind of plate, almost two millennia ago. I fought back a surge of terrible laughter. It felt momentarily as madness must feel to the suffering lunatic and so I pushed it inside of me as completely as I could.

Frankenstein took the proffered cup and saucer, and thanked me. Mrs Greene did the same.

"I dare say that this is all rather unexpected," said the man from Geneva. "I cannot believe you ever truly imagined that we would come back."

I took a sip of my own tea. All three of us were standing. The scene seemed too tense for any one of us to sit.

"I think," I said, "that we all believed you had fled for good, leaving behind your new… creation."

"It is true," Frankenstein replied, "that my reaction to seeing the boy was not entirely as it ought to have been. Nor was that of Mrs Greene. Yet time has changed us both. We see things now in a different light. We have travelled much and we have enriched ourselves and I think that we both have come to understand our place in the world a little better."

I took another sip of tea and asked, as mildly as I was able: "What do you want?"

My two visitors exchanged a look of dark understanding. It was the lady who replied. "We want the child," she said.

This I had not foreseen. "In heaven's name, why?"

"He is ours." An outsider who did not know the true story would have thought her entirely sincere, at least if they had not spied the lights of distant madness dancing in her eyes. "We made him, you see, Victor and I."

"It is my understanding," I replied, "that the poor being in question was stitched and darned together out of indiscriminate parts and somehow imbued with life. That he has become so well-mannered as he largely has is due entirely to the good custodianship of his father."

Frankenstein interjected. "How interesting that you would take that line. Is it, then, your contention that Mr Nathaniel Greene may be considered an able and a dutiful parent?"

"Outside," I said, "when you stood upon my threshold you said that you had a favour that you wished to ask of me. I suggest that you ask me that favour now and that you leave."

"It is a very simple thing," smiled Victor Frankenstein. "And that is for you to do nothing. That is, to take no practical step to avert the course of what we mean to do tonight."

"That, sir," I said briskly, "sounds like a Devil's bargain if ever I heard one."

Alice placed one hand upon his arm. With the fingers of the other, she brushed that hand of mine which held my cup. "Please," she said. "I can explain."

"Then do so."

"We have tried to get the boy back already. We have written to Nathaniel. I tried myself to visit with him. Against my better judgement, for I always did despise the man, I even persuaded the Judge to help us yet he too was firmly rebuffed. I have investigated a legal solution but such a thing is not possible, the parentage being, at least in the eyes of the courts, a complicated thing."

"Then," I said, "the matter would seem to me to be quite settled. Whatever manner of being it is that you created up in that Hall in '43 I do not believe that there is any better personage to watch over it than Nathaniel Greene, with, I flatter myself, my own occasional assistance."

Frankenstein tutted, as might a schoolmaster about to demonstrate a point. "Yet I fear that the good people of Crispin Rye might not be entirely in agreement with you. For there have been incidents, have there not?"

"Rumours," I said. "Nothing more than that. Believe me, country people talk."

Another smile uncurled itself upon the lips of the physician. "Schoolchildren startled in fields by a lumbering human shape. Livestock driven half-mad by fear without any obvious source and whispers, yes, of worse still. Bloodstains in the forest. Injuries without explanation. That gang of robbers the year before last, who languish still in a state of perpetual terror. And then, quite naturally, there are fears that such events are in a process of escalation. Fears, shared by many, that the people of this village are living with a monster in their midst, whose behaviour grows ever more unruly." He seemed pleased by the sound of his own recitation.

"This may be true," I allowed, "but I fail to see how it strengthens your case over the guardianship of Mr Greene."

"A boy should be with his mother," murmured the woman.

Frankenstein raised a hand to silence her. "The villagers' dismay will allow me to raise a mob. I have some experience of mobs. We will take the little Creature by force. We will spirit him away and all will be as it was once here was in Crispin Rye."

"I see," I said. "And I am to do nothing?"

Frankenstein smiled placidly. "Nothing at all."

I gazed at them, these terrible visitors. "How can I possibly assent to that? How can I stand by and permit a riot to take place in my own parish while I drowse by the fireside like an old maid? No, sir! No, madam!"

Victor Frankenstein sighed heavily and said to Alice: "I told you that he would be as he is. I know his kind of old."

"We had to try," said Mrs Greene. She looked back at her friend and, I suspect, he who was her master. He gave her a single nod, an inclination of his head almost too subtle to be seen.

Then, without further warning, she was upon me. She threw herself at me, sending me flying to the floor, cup and saucer shattering noisily upon the ground. I cried out, more in shock than from pain. She bared her teeth at me like an animal and hissed.

From somewhere above me floated the mirthless laughter of the Genevese physician. I called out words of protestation, the details of which I do not now recollect. I struggled, for the woman was surprisingly strong. Then, to my horror, she reached into her bodice and, in a single sinuous motion, drew out a long gleaming blade. I fear that at this I truly did scream.

Then the blade was soaring down towards me. I knew pain of the most searing kind. Then, mercifully, surging like an incoming tide, came darkness.

When I awoke, it was to the discovery of three remarkable things. The first was that night had fallen (evidently I had lain in that terrible swoon for some five or six hours). The second was that I could hear in the distance the sounds of uproar and screaming. The third, and most extraordinary, thing was that I was not alone in the chamber.

A figure was bent down low above me. I knew at once the nature of his identity for I had, after all, seen him myself not long ago, if at a distance.

Yet to see him in such proximity was to be struck with awe. Tall he was, and yellow-eyed, his dark hair lustrous and his teeth quite white. There was wisdom in his gaze, kindness, pity and — a thing which I shall never forget so long as I draw breath — an abiding disappointment at the ways of the world. There were visible scars upon him, yet he possessed a quality of strange beauty.

He had been busying himself with my ruined left hand. With a jolt of disgust, I understood that Mrs Greene had removed two fingers entirely. The loss of blood must have been considerable. Yet the Creature seemed to have staunched the wound and to have applied a rough bandage.

"You wake," he said. His voice was a weird, sonorous thing. "I have done that which I am able. But I am no physician."

"Thank you." I struggled upright and the Creature helped me to my feet. "I owe you a great debt."

The being towered over me and I felt, in spite of his obvious kindness, a frisson of fear at the size and power of him.

"No doubt," he said. "But if you wish to help your friend, you must hurry. The crisis is upon us now."

I found that I tottered a little upon my feet and that my vision swam. The Creature placed a steadying hand upon me.

"What has happened?" I asked.

"He who created me did as he threatened. He raised a mob from the village and set off to the Hall to confront its ruined master. He and the woman wanted the boy."

"And did they succeed?"

The grim features of the being before me arranged themselves uneasily into a smile. "They did not."

As if in answer to an invocation, the boy, Adam, stepped out of the shadows. He must have been standing there, still and silent, watching as the older Creature did his best to repair me. With a tremor of realisation, I recalled my first meeting with the boy and understood this final encounter to be its mirror.

"This…" said the child, in a voice that seemed to me to be clearer and more confident than ever before, "this is my brother."

"Yes," I said. "I suppose he is."

"I am to take the boy," the Creature said, looking once towards the door – a gesture which in a human being might almost have looked like nervousness. "I will keep him safe for now. Your friend Mr Greene and I have come to an arrangement."

"Indeed? And where is he now?"

"At the Hall. The mob surrounded him. He bade me fly and so I did. He has pledged to join us later. And now I must away. We have to reach a place of safety apart from my creator. I see now what I feared was true – that in spite of his fine words, he has not mended his ways, nor shall he ever."

I looked at him and saw in his face a complete earnestness of purpose allied to an unparalleled will.

"I will go to the Hall," I said, "and do what I may, while you keep the boy safe."

From somewhere far away, there came cries of horror and triumph.

"You must hurry," said the Creature and we all three turned, meaning to go out into the night, only for the door to the parlour to be thrown open and an aged figure walk in with a pistol stretched out before him and a satchel slung still about his shoulder.

"Wait!" cried Victor Frankenstein and the moment was so delirious, so emphatic in its drama that it scarcely seemed real. Mad laughter bubbled up within me once again. This soon was dampened by a glance at the visages of the two old opponents and the realisation that we were trapped now – the Greene boy and I – in a room with the two most dangerous men in Christendom.

The fury in the eyes of the man from Geneva was matched by the dull anguish in the Creature's gaze.

"How dare you?" said Victor. "Yet again you have seized what is mine. Demon!"

"The boy is not yours," said the Creature. "You relinquished all right to him as you did once to me. Coward!"

Frankenstein stepped closer to the monster, his pistol outstretched. The child and I were altogether helpless, mere observers to a drama which had begun long decades past.

"I believed…" the Creature said in its slow and deliberate fashion, "that you had changed. In the ice I dreamed of you and in the mud beneath the city also. I felt regret. Remorse. And so I sought you out. I found you incarcerated. Penned up with the mad. And I set you free." Frankenstein nodded, his face gleaming now with perspiration, the hand which held the gun trembling.

"You told me that you had changed," the Creature went on. "That you had learned hard lessons and that you were prepared to make amends."

"And I did!" Frankenstein protested. "I thanked you then and I thank you now for my freedom from that asylum. I have done much. To Mrs Greene, I gave her heart's desire. New life! You see? A child of her own!"

As he spoke, I felt, to my surprise, the rough hand of the child slip into mine and his uneven voice declare: "Hurry, sir... quick now... let us escape while we can..."

With great and elaborate care, the two of us stepped around the edges of that little parlour and towards the door.

The two main players in the tragedy took not the slightest notice of us, so entirely engrossed were they in one another.

"Seven years I gave you," said Creature to creator. "Seven years to make amends before I would return. That was my promise. That was our agreement. And this – this horror – is what I discover!"

He advanced upon his old master. The creator stood firm; immovable object and unstoppable force. Victor Frankenstein snarled at the approach of his Creature, his face a mask of rage, turned in a trice into something more animal than man. He fired.

The Creature roared, yet still he lumbered onwards, his fingers reaching for the man's neck.

I could watch no more. The boy tugged in desperation at my hand and then we were beyond the parlour and racing towards the front door. Behind us, I heard the revolver fire again.

The boy and I careered out of the house and into the street, fleeing in horror and disgust. The road was quiet. In the distance was smoke and the sounds of voices raised in anger. Fieldwick Hall was in flames.

Pain flared up in my wretched left hand. I took a breath to steady my nerves.

"What now?" I asked, whether to myself, to the boy or to the Lord Almighty I knew not.

Yet when I looked down I saw that the child had vanished. All was silent. There was no noise in the house behind me. Then, from the edge of the village, I heard a scream.

Feeling certain that this now was my purpose and my mission, I ran towards the Hall to see if I might not yet rescue some good from this long, dark night.

In this, as you will be all too sadly aware, I failed. That long day was to end in tragedy.

You must understand that I did not lightly leave the boy, only that I believed my efforts would be better spent at the Hall than in search of that little creature whom, I knew, was adept, at the very least, at hiding.

I ran for only a short while. My injuries still roared in my left hand and I grew exhausted. What had once been a pleasant walk from the heart of the village to the Hall became, that night, an ordeal.

After a time, I came upon the first of the villagers returning to their homes. In a sequence of hours which are amongst the most indelible of my life, I find that it is their faces which I most readily recall. They seemed dazed and bewildered, more as though they were stumbling from the site of some disaster than from a place they had themselves attacked.

Many cast their eyes down at the sight of me as if my presence made them obscurely ashamed.

Mr Barrendale, the poacher, was the exception.

He called out with glee: "We've done it, Reverend! We've pulled out the poison by the root!"

I only looked at him in reply. If he were expecting his

fellows to break into cheers or expressions of argument then none came. Instead, the people of Crispin Rye simply trickled by me, white and blank of expression, like mourners at a funeral for one who was taken years before their time.

I found their silence to be obscurely dreadful, somehow worse than it would have been to hear whoops and ululations of victory. I chose to ignore them and simply ran on.

At last, I reached the Hall to find it all but abandoned. In places, it still smouldered but the fires had been, by and large, extinguished. There were signs of violence done and much visible damage (some of this you saw for yourself, Mr Malone, not so very long ago), yet it was clear that the mob had done its worst and passed over.

As I approached, a figure stepped from the front door and raised a hand in sardonic greeting.

"Judge," I said, for it was indeed that rubicund and mendacious gentleman. He was grinning broadly as he strode towards me.

"Been a long time coming all this!" he said. "Long time, Reverend. Years and years!"

My creed is one of peace and forbearance but at the sight of his round red face I felt an all but irresistible urge to swing the first punch of my adult life.

Indeed, I might even have done so were it not for what I heard then, from one of those outbuildings on the periphery of the Hall, a thin, wheedling cry of absolute devastation. Without looking back, I ran towards the source of it. The Judge did not follow and it is perhaps as well for both of us that I have not seen that treacherous personage since.

There is not so very much left now for me to tell. The source of the cry you may already have guessed was Nathaniel Greene.

I found him in a hut which had at one time been meant for the storage of various agricultural implements and which smelt now of damp grass and sawdust.

Crouched in the gloom, there was something piteously canine in his posture. He rocked back and forth upon his haunches.

"Where is my boy?" he asked, although I was by no means certain that he understood to whom he was speaking and that he was not merely addressing the air. "They tried to take him, you see. Tried to seize him but he was too quick and too clever. Special boy, that one. Special."

"I have seen him," I said. "Adam is safe and protected. His brother came for him and watches over him."

This was not quite a lie though neither was it the complete truth. If you wonder now, Mr Malone, why I could not face Greene again in his cell at Newgate then this is at least a partial explanation.

I do not know the location of the child or even if he still lives.

I pray daily that he does.

"Good," breathed Nathaniel. "That is good." He chuckled, a hideous sound in the dark. "You know who was the worst of them in the end? The most vicious in her assault upon me to wrest my boy from my embrace? None of the villagers, mad and bloodthirsty though they were. Not the Genevese physician for all his subtlety and guile. No, it was her. Always her."

With his left hand, he gestured to a shadow in the corner of the hut.

I had taken it to be some shrouded implement or other but now a fresh, horrific possibility occurred to me.

"There was good in her once," Greene said. "When we first met. I ought to have nurtured it. I see that now. I ought to have listened and to have helped. But you know how it is, over time, between a man and a woman. You know how things languish and… congeal."

"Nathaniel," I said gently. "Nathaniel, what have you done?"

Suspecting that I knew the answer to my own question, I walked towards the object.

"I knew I should have been a better husband," he went on. "Knew I should have been kind… Faithful, of course, and true. Yet what she became, not her own fault or mine. It was him, don't you see? He who corrupted her."

I reached the object. In the gloom, I looked down. There was light, just enough, from the moon to make out the truth of it.

"I had no choice. Don't you understand? What mother would she have been? My boy… My poor boy… There. There she lies. You see her mottled face? Her staring eyes? There she is, Reverend. There lies Frankenstein's monster!"

I forced myself to look.

Poor Alice Greene. Her body was broken and lifeless on the ground. There were dark marks upon her neck from where her husband had throttled the last breath from her.

"Nathaniel…" I said. "What is this terrible – this unforgivable – thing you have done?"

He loosed a moan of absolute despair.

And in that unlighted place I stood and, though my voice was tremulous and lacking in any passion, I began to recite the words of the twenty-third Psalm: "The Lord is my Shepherd, I shall not want. He maketh me to lie down in green pastures…"

And so, Mr Malone, you know now the truth of it. I often wish that Fieldwick Hall had burned entirely to the ground that night. Indeed, after the arrest and trial I have thought of taking matters into my own hands and turning arsonist. Yet something stayed my hand and bade me keep away. Something warned me off. Yes, perhaps there is some truth, after all, in the old tales.

I pray often. I pray for the sinner, Nathaniel, for the soul of his wife, for the well-being of that weird, misshapen boy. I pray for your friend also, sir, for I fear that some fresh shadow has fallen also over him.

Please do not reply to this missive. I have no more to say to you about any of it, only to God and, even then, I am far from certain that He is listening.

May the Lord bless you and keep you, Mr Malone. I mean this very week to retire and leave this place. I have done enough – too much. And now I must go elsewhere. It is my fervent suggestion that you and Mr Crowe do the same. You are an American, are you not? Return home, sir. Put the Atlantic in the path of impending catastrophe! To have anything further to do with this black tragedy is to invite in further wickedness of the worst kind. Be strong, sir, I beg of you. Be stronger than

I have been. I ought never to have shown you and your friend the Hall.

Who knows now what evil influence guided my hand and waved away my misgivings that day? Who knows what bade me usher you over the threshold?

May God forgive me in the end.
Yours sincerely,
Reverend C. W. Leigh-Stanley

PART SEVEN

THE PERSONAL TESTIMONY OF JESSE MALONE

(continued)

I

Now, I read this long letter from the preacher with a sense of ever-increasing dread. All that I had feared seemed to me now to have been horribly consolidated.

For too long had I nursed my secret anxieties and my vague, formless concerns. For too long had I tried to persuade myself that I was doing little more than jumping at shadows. Fretting unduly over what was real and what was not.

No longer. Upon reading the priest's tale, I rose quickly, flung on a coat and hat and, to the bemusement of Mrs Armitage, fled the confines of my apartment. Outside, in the midst of the London swirl and bustle, I forced myself onwards and gave myself no opportunity to hesitate or turn back. I flagged down a cab, urging its driver to take me at once, and without thought for the well-being of his horses, to Pilate Court.

As we journeyed, I thought of all I had read, of the strange, crooked child, of the Genevese physician, of the Creature who stalked and of he who waited still in Newgate to face justice for the slaying of his tormented wife.

I felt certain that some terrible reaction had been set in motion, the full consequences of which could not yet be guessed at, and which might not be seen for many months or even years to come.

Yet, somehow, when I reached that familiar structure, I knew also that Hubert Crowe had gone. I felt it on some deep, instinctive level. I knocked and the door was opened almost at once, not by my friend but by that cracked lady who I had seen there a time or two before, she who spoke in an accent not so very distant from my own.

"He's gone, Mr Malone. He's gone and he left no note."

She gave me a wide smile. I fear I was unmannered. I pushed past her and went inside. The door to my friend's apartment was unlocked yet within the place was quite bare, devoid of furniture or a single possession, filled only with dust and memory.

I emerged to find the old woman standing on the threshold of the Crowe residence and examining me with baleful, half-crazed eyes.

"He left nothing?" I asked. "Nothing at all? No message?"

She looked at me with great disdain. "He said you'd probably visit here eventually."

"Oh? And did he leave any instructions for that eventuality?"

"He said, Mr Malone, sir, that I should say to you that you know where he's gone now and that you weren't to follow him there. He said he wouldn't welcome you. He said it's over and done. He said to forget about him and live your own life." She grinned a grin of sharp yellow teeth. "But can you do that, Mr Malone? Can you do that, sir?" She peeled back her lips still further and winked. "Can you truly leave him be?"

II

Returning home to Clerkenwell, my mind in uproar, I spied a fellow selling newspapers on the street adjacent to my own. He was scarcely more than a boy, red-headed, his face a mass of spots which spoke of survival from smallpox. The copies of his publication were in a tottering stack beside him and he seemed to handle them almost tenderly, evidently caring deeply for his wares. I had seen a man on Piccadilly selling tortoises once – they seemed to him to be as much companions as they were wares – and I was reminded of him in that moment, seeing that boy with his newspapers.

Though all of this detail was to flee from my faculties when I heard him cry out the news of the day: "Murderer dead! Wife-killer dead in his cell! Dead a day before he was doomed to hang!"

He was delivering this news with a troubling kind of relish. I stopped him.

"This man," I said, "this murderer... was his name Nathaniel Greene?"

"None other." The boy grinned savagely.

"How did he die?" I asked. "Was it by his own hand?"

The young man shrugged. "Buy a copy from me, sir, and find out! Shame, though, a man like that – anyone who'd kill his own wife – a man like that deserves to dangle from the end of a long rope, don't you think, sir? Dangle and dance!"

I said nothing, not being sure exactly what I ought to think, but I bought a paper all the same and hurried home with it.

The facts were clear enough. Nathaniel Greene had been found dead in his cell that afternoon. There were no obvious signs of violence, nor had he received any visitors for days. The report did not speculate as to the cause of his demise though I dare say the correspondent had not seen what I had seen – the grim, guttering light in the eyes of that murderer. Is it possible for a man to perish from shame and regret? If so, then Greene was most certainly that man. Had he cheated justice by way of this early expiration? Or is there some greater consequence awaiting him?

All is uncertainty as I write. Nothing coheres and the shadows that have fallen across us all seem only to grow darker.

I read that article over and over in the course of that long night. I wished for guidance but could not imagine to which authority I would turn. Where Crowe might have his cards and Leigh-Stanley his God, I now had nothing at all save for myself and that was soon to prove grossly insufficient.

I lay awake for many hours, rehearsing in my mind all those very terrible events of which I had been told and trying my utmost to understand how they were linked together. I take no pleasure in admitting that I thought also of the old woman's words on the threshold of Pilate Court when she had all but goaded me into going after my friend, Mr Crowe.

Friend? Was that truly what he was? Many and various thoughts passed through my mind and I do not shrink from admitting that I considered the path of cowardice. Then I remembered the grateful face of the Olney boy and I knew that such a path would never allow me any rest.

By dawn, my choice was made.

III

On the next day, I made the journey once again to the village of Crispin Rye. It took many hours and it was twilight when I arrived. I had spent the trip in a state of constant, gnawing agitation.

I did not go either to the inn (too many questions) or to

the vicarage (by now abandoned), but straight to the Hall which I felt certain was now the possession of Mr Crowe. The place struck me as different than on my earlier visit. Knowing what I knew by then of the nature of the storm that had passed through the village earlier this year lent it all a different hue.

At the station, I had engaged a dog-cart and driver and the fields and woodlands seemed silent and watchful as we passed by, just a dot in that stark landscape. They seemed the perfect setting for further tragedy.

When I reached the Hall I saw, to my subtle horror, that the place was all lit up. Each window blazed. There were also copious signs of building work as the burned and wormy structure of the place was being repaired. There was evidence also of certain troubling new buildings and extensions, suggestive of enlargement and expansion of a house which, like Leigh-Stanley, I now dearly wished had been razed to the ground.

I asked my driver to wait for me and told him that I may be emerging shortly with another, even if I had to drag him bodily from that benighted site.

I went to the threshold. I knocked. A terrible minute of expectation. Then the door was opened.

Hubert Crowe stood before me, large as life. He seemed tired. "You ought not to have come," was all that he said at the sight of me.

"My God," I said, the words surging from me. "What have you done? Please, this is no place for you. Come back with me to London."

Crowe seemed distant in his manner, faraway and already half-lost. "The cards were clear," he said. "This is where I have to be. The Hall had called to me, you see. And not just to me…"

It was only then that I realised the dreadful totality of my loss for another person now emerged from somewhere deeper in the house. I knew him at once, at first sight, for had I not heard his description often enough?

The elderly Genevese physician was now very frail indeed. His old body was failing him. He was, however, dressed in clothes of evident expense. He stepped up behind my friend and brushed his left hand against his shoulder. "Go inside," he said. "Dear Hubert. And permit me, please, to speak awhile with our visitor."

Crowe seemed grateful and nodded with a canine happiness that seemed altogether uncharacteristic of him. "Please leave me alone," he said to me – the last words he ever spoke to me – and there was no doubt at all that he meant them.

"You must be Mr Malone?" asked the physician.

"I am indeed," I said as, behind him, Crowe disappeared into the house. From within, I heard voices, both male and female.

The madman before me gave me a small, tight smile, that of an official dismissing an underling. "I think that you really ought to leave now," he said. "The new owner of Fieldwick Hall does not wish to have you here."

To underscore these words, he brought out a long, sleek knife and brandished it with a surgeon's precision.

I did my best, yet I flinched just the same. I knew I could overpower him easily yet the sheer potency of the man, still burning through his decrepit frame, kept me in my place. "What do you want?" I asked, sounding plaintive and defeated. "What exactly do you want?"

"Only to continue my work. Only to see what might yet be achieved. With now the assistance of a new friend. Please leave us, Mr Malone. You heard Mr Crowe's request. There was in it to be heard no ambiguity. And pray, sir, do not come back."

He moved the knife before my face. I rocked backwards slightly on my feet. He chuckled at the sight of it. "Go," he said.

Then, to my great shame, I did exactly as he asked. I turned and I did not look back. I went to my waiting coach and I fled once again from that cursed village. I made haste back to London, all the while able to hear nothing else, ringing in my ears, save for the terrible, resounding laughter of Victor Frankenstein.

I am not wanted. I am not wanted here.

All that I can imagine now is to leave, to obey the word of the old Reverend and return, at last, to America.

It is to that end that I must work tirelessly.

Tirelessly!*

---

* Here the document is concluded. I believe the date to have been August 27th, 1850. Yet Malone seems to have been a driven man. He could not set his pen aside for long. And five days later he commenced the composition of a diary.

PART EIGHT

THE JOURNAL OF JESSE MALONE

September 1st, 1850*

Why start a diary? Why now, when I have already made a full and frank account of all of my recent experiences at the side of poor Hubert Crowe? There is surely nothing more to add. I have made a clean breast of it. I have visited with him and can do nothing now to help him. To even attempt to do so would be to risk my own life, my sanity or still worse. I have decided I must look to the future. I must take care of myself.

To that end, I have booked passage on the RMS *Sanctity*. We sail eleven days from now, on 12th September. I find that I am counting the very hours. Such desperation to be away from London I have never known before. Who would ever have imagined this fierce new eagerness to be free of the old country and back in the land of my birth?

I told Mrs Armitage of my decision this afternoon and she was distressed. She tried to enfold me in an embrace and I had to skirt the very boundaries of decorum in order to shoo her away.

September 2nd, 1850

Much business to be dealt with today at the Assembly. I flatter myself to think that I have become somewhat essential to that

---

* At this point the calm, well-ordered hand in which Malone's testimony has, until now, been written starts to degenerate, growing wilder and more desperate as the days go by.

organisation and that I will be sorely missed when I depart. I have written also to that gentleman in New York who has taken care of the family estate in my long absence. His name, as I recall, is Coenraads, though I am far from certain I spelled it correctly in my correspondence. Ten days left now. I busy myself with farewells and with administration though I fear that there will not be enough of either to take up all my time before I leave these shores. I fear that my mind is wandering to other things. Other places. Other personages also.

September 3rd, 1850

Today I was reduced to walking the streets of London, in an effort to distract myself. Yet everywhere reminds me of him, and of what I have done by my abandonment of him. Out of some mixture of weakness and naive hope I even tried to visit with a police detective and enlist his aid in what has been done to my friend. The gentleman's name was Miller and he was friendly enough. I think he thought me mad, though, and he was most insistent that no provable crime has been committed by Victor Frankenstein and that Crowe's request was quite plain. I could not stand the calm sympathy of the man for long and so I fled out into the street, ending our conversation without the slightest courtesy. No doubt this served only to confirm his view of me.

I find it hard to sleep. Mrs Armitage is concerned and she has urged me in the strongest terms to stay in England and, by extension, in her care. This I have refused, without ever saying quite why.

September 4th, 1850

I find myself looking at train timetables, seeing how a return to Crispin Rye might be done. I wonder if I could sneak into the village, like a thief in the night, how I might sweep Crowe away from that malign actor who is (though he seems not to realise it) his gaoler in all but name. Could it be done? Would I need help? Of course I would for I shrink from violence of any kind. Could I hire some men to act as my protectors and aides? As the Judge did once, only for them all to be chased away by a handful of mysterious words from the man from Geneva?

If I still had my complete faith I would pray. Yet that seems altogether without point now, though I cannot wholly reject the notion that there is some unseen mechanism to the universe, some secret clockwork. Perhaps I should wait? Yes. Wait for a sign. Still only six days before I have to leave.

September 5th, 1850

I fear I am losing all confidence in my own faculties. Last night my dreams did not seem to me to be dreams at all, so real did they appear and so full of pungent detail.

I emerged from the darkness of slumber and opened my eyes. Yet (in my dream, if such it was) I was not in bed any longer but lying upon a rough, uneven surface which seemed also somehow to be swaying. It took me a moment to realise what it was: something like wicker, something like plaited wood. And as to the swaying? With all the logic of the night-time vision I recognised it then as being the basket of a great hot-air balloon.

In the moment of dreaming, this did not surprise me and I simply got to my feet, just as though I were merely rising first thing in the morning. The surface beneath me creaked and swayed but not unpleasantly. I gripped the high corners of the basket that was being borne aloft by that vast balloon above my head and looked tentatively over the side. I was indeed high above the world. We were travelling at some speed, moved ever onwards by the aeronautical currents, and I saw below me, with a dizzying understanding which might in real life have been a moment of terror but which in the dream-world was merely startling. There it was – the intersection of land and sea. White cliffs. The surging ocean beyond. We were leaving England, I could see that, and heading to parts unknown.

I realised then that I was not alone in the balloon. There were two others. I recognised them both from the plentiful descriptions I had received: a tall, shambling Creature with yellow eyes and, by his side, his crooked younger brother.

In my dream, I could not speak. Yet they seemed to know me.

I saw the Creature place an arm around his sibling and draw him to his side. He turned his eyes upon me and I saw there two things – a look of reassurance but one also of warning. He opened his mouth. His voice was extraordinary.

"Do not," he said, "do not go to the—"

Though I know it in my heart I did not hear the final word of his sentence. I woke then in my own bed, gasping for breath, covered in perspiration, trembling from the intensity of my dream.

It was, I am sure, nothing more than a phantasy. Yet I cannot forget it. Each moment of it stays with me even as I try to pack and prepare for my long voyage. Not long now! Just a week.

September 6th, 1850

My head is full.

No funeral for Nathaniel Greene, I see.

Another long and painful scene with Mrs Armitage.

To avoid her disapproving gaze I have taken to wandering the streets again, in spite of the heat. I have had too many warnings now to even consider action to rescue my friend? Have I not? What more could be sent to me as a sign?

September 7th, 1850

Today, a sign.

An envelope in the post, marked as from the county of Norfolk. No message on the inside, no note. Only a card, one I knew of old. The Mountain Gate. A new journey, new beginnings. The card which Hubert Crowe once said, on only our second meeting, would define our shared future.

I have to go.

Yes, I have to go back.

September 8th, 1850

I write these words on the train that is moving once again into the east of this little nation. I hope I will live to write more than this but for now this must suffice. I am to go again to Crispin Rye. I am to rescue my friend, Hubert Crowe, from the clutches of the madman Frankenstein and I will take him with me to America. We will be happy there, and safe, and away from all the horrors of the old world.

Later.

It was dark when I arrived at Crispin Rye tonight. The vicarage still lies empty, awaiting the new holder of that office. The whole place has, even more than before, a stealthy, watchful air. I have taken a room once again at The Mariner's Rest. No-one will speak to me (to think that I was concerned before about a surfeit of questions!). I had half-hoped that I might raise some small militia to raid the Hall and free my friend – certainly, it sounds as though Victor Frankenstein himself was able to achieve this not so very long ago. Yet nobody will even meet my eye. I will do what I must alone. Though I have come armed this time.

September 9th, 1850

Morning. And time to do what I must. I have managed to prise free a few unguarded words from the publican. He tells me that the Hall has been unusually busy in recent days but that it has since fallen quiet again. There have been visitors, he says, and much coming and going. More than that he will not say. I tell him where I am going and that he is to raise the alarm if I am not returned by nightfall. He only grunted in acknowledgement and hurried away. So alone it must be. To the Hall.

Later.[*]

---

[*] Needless to say, the hand here is especially wild and desperate. God knows under what extremities of human experience it was written.

No. No, I cannot – I will not – accept it. Not what I've seen. Not what I saw... saw in his eyes. Dear God, his eyes! I will not think of it, let alone write it down here, lest I go mad. I must keep going. Yes. I must keep my gaze on the horizon. And I must not think of that face, of the sights that I saw in the outbuilding at the Hall in Crispin Rye, of the awful sound of that repeated tapping.

October 5th, 1850[*]

A day away from America and home. The voyage has been good for my spirits. The distance it has provided me has been restorative to my state of mind. I have lost myself often in the sight of the sea. Dare I now put down what I saw in that benighted Hall? Dare I set out how I approached it and found it empty and deserted? How I went from room to room, calling the name of my friend? How, with increasing boldness but also with a heavy feeling of disquiet, I walked through it all and found the detritus of what looked to me like a sequence of disgusting experiments? How, emerging at last into the open air, I heard a noise emanating from one of the outhouses?

Dare I write of my careful circling around that structure? Of how I heard from within a sound of tapping, like stone upon wood? Of how I went as close as I dared and called out,

---

[*] The hand here is a little more stable than in the preceding entry. It seems likely that in the intervening stretch of days, in which time Mr Malone evidently boarded the RMS *Sanctity* to America, that he was able to claw back a little of his sanity, if only temporarily so.

once more, the name of my friend? And then of how I heard from within a moan of distant recognition?

Perhaps. Perhaps I could write of these things. But nothing more. Nothing further. Not now.

October 6th, 1850

At last, today the voyage ended and I am home again, after all these long years. I feel a little relieved to be here but not, perhaps, to the degree that I ought. There is something at my back, a kind of shadow... Memories only, surely, however recent they may happen to be? I will find somewhere to stay for tonight and enjoy a night of quiet anonymity. In the morning, I will discover Mr Coenraads and begin the slow return to my old life.

Later.

I write this in an agreeable room in Manhattan. I have checked in under a false name. I have already dozed and eaten, eaten and dozed. I start to see something of myself again.

Perhaps now I should set it down? As a kind of exorcism?

Yes, perhaps I shall. Perhaps I will write just a little more of what I found in that outbuilding by the Hall. Dare I? Who knows, in the future, who might yet read these words?

Very well. Something more of the truth of it.

The tapping continued as I walked to the door. Someone was surely inside. It was no mere animal – the groan had already made that clear.

The door was unlocked though, when I pushed it, it would not open. I had to be firm and push it with force before I could steal into the room.

At my feet was a dead body in a state of absolute butchery and ruination. It took me a moment to recognise who it must be: the old Genevese physician himself, Victor Frankenstein reduced after all this time to offal.

He had been dead for days. That much was clear. He could not have made the sounds which had drawn me to this place.

And then I saw it, something in the shadows, a thing that was shackled... that groaned and stretched... a monstrous thing that knew my name!

"Malone... Jesse..." The voice was a wretched, grinding thing.

I went closer. I saw the obscenity of that shambling beast. To my unutterable horror I saw that I recognised the bulk of its being as having belonged to that of my dear friend, Hubert Crowe. Though there had been... alterations also. And, dear God, *additions*.

It lurched upwards. It reached for me, that patchwork new Creature.

And then I saw it. I saw the nature of its eyes.

Enough now. Bedtime. Sleep. And tomorrow – a new beginning.

October 7th, 1850

Dear God, no. How can this be? Am I mad? If I am not now I feel certain that it must be merely a matter of time. How has it done this thing? How has it followed me here?

I must lose myself amongst the masses. I must run. I must

hide. Was it with me the whole time? Aboard the ship? Watching and biding its time?

For I cannot face it again, the thing that moves about the world with unholy purpose. That which stalks me, which dreams of vengeance, which plots and schemes and cultivates its crazed designs. That monstrous thing which wears my old friend's body, yes, but which looks out at all creation with the eyes of another... the cunning, evil eyes of Victor Frankenstein.*

---

* The journal ends here. I can no find no further trace or record of Mr Malone until my father's discovery of him on the evening of April 13th, 1852.

༺❦༻

I do not believe my father was ever quite the same again after he set aside that volume which you have just read, late on the evening of April fourteenth, 1852. It was as though, in the hours that he had sat with it, he had been exposed to some infection, one which seemed at first to lie dormant inside him but which was, in truth, already hard at work within his system.

He left the bar that night, bade a strictly neighbourly goodnight to its mistress and came home to my mother, with Malone's scrapbook held tightly under his arm. He did not tell her of its contents – not then – but he stowed it safely in a little compartment beneath the stairs in which we deposited such few valuables as we possessed. He went into my room next and kissed me as I slept. Then he comforted my mother and let her sleep on, while sleep did not come at all easily to him. How could it when the world was filled with such horrors?

There are many who might simply have dismissed the document as a hoax or, more likely, as the complicated and inventive ramblings of an unwell man. Yet my pa, although I believed him when he told me that he tried his best to do so, could not set the thing aside nor could he reject it as a simple forgery. It had taken up residence, you see, in his imagination. He never travelled to Britain himself but he always said that he could picture that cursed little village of Crispin Rye just as well as though he knew it intimately, as though he had walked through its green and shadowed avenues, through the fields, the patch of woodland, the blasted structure of Fieldwick Hall.

For a long time, however, life went on just as ever it did, with all of its many surprises, crises and moments of fleeting happiness. The death in custody of Jesse Malone was hushed up easily enough and I dare say that Mr Coenraads had more than a hand in this. Twenty years have gone by since then and the Malone fortune still exists, funnelled by that selfsame Dutch gentleman into a multifarious and most productive company, the name of which you would surely recognise if I ever told it to you.

If you know the history of the New York police force, you will already be able to guess that the time immediately following the Malone affair was more than usually difficult and bloody. There were riots on the streets in 1857 after the creation of the Metropolitan Police, which still rules over the city to this day. My father was there, right in the thick of it, and he had many an interesting tale to tell about it all. Not only concerning the creation of the force and the battles against those plentiful gangs who held sway over many of the streets, but a sequence of interesting cases too – murders and abductions, civic warfare, the horrible secrets of powerful men.

Though all of these must wait for another day should I survive to write it. For I have a particular purpose in the collation and presentation of this volume which I shall now make clear.

My father died two years ago and he died raving. No, not quite raving, that is unfair, but most certainly in a state which I thought then to be one of extreme eccentricity, even perhaps on the very borderlands of lunacy.

I well recall the last time I saw him. My mother we had

lost in an accident in '66 and my father had lived alone ever since, not in the place where they had raised me but in a stark bachelor's apartment in Brooklyn. There had even, since his widowing, been several lady-friends but I never cared to meet any of them nor did my father speak of those women after his initial attempts to do so had been greeted by me with a kind of stern indifference. A rather childish disapproval, I see now, carried out no doubt in the memory of my mother.

At this time, I lived not far from him. I had not followed him into the police force myself but had sought out quite a different profession, being employed by the university as a junior tutor in American History. It was easy enough work and I enjoyed it, though it was not my father's world at all and it seemed to place another barrier between the two of us, now two men, one old and the other young, without the restraining influence of my mother to keep things civil between us. Not that we had fallen out since her death, or even anything like it – only that there was frost and a little distance. I regretted it even at the time and I have regretted it still more since his passing.

Yet there was one matter on which we were able to discourse quite happily, one area of common ground. This, of course, was the manuscript which you yourself have now read, the Malone documents which had been in my father's possession by then for fourteen years.

I think that a part of him always imagined (or half-feared, or half-hoped) that someone in authority would arrive to take it from him one day, either from the force or, more likely, some emissary from Mr Coenraads. But this day never came. Nobody ever missed the scrapbook because nobody still living knew that it had ever existed.

And so it stayed with my father in the years since the death of its author, always working on him, sinking its claws deeper and deeper into his imagination and his processes of reason. He told me the story in full not long after the death of my mother – it made a welcome change from conversations about funeral arrangements and all that stifled, unspoken grief – and he gave me (he trusted me) with the scrapbook itself two days after we had put her in the ground and said our last farewells.

This seemed to mark a new stage in both of our lives. He seemed to long for company in his obsession. I did not wish to join him in it but I did agree to sit down and read the thing for the first time, having heard until then only hints and cryptic titbits.

In that first full reading, I could see something at least of what had drawn him in, of the strange gravity of the thing. I remember my father asking me a few nights later when he came to call, still dressed in black for the death of his wife, just exactly what I made of it all.

"Expect you think it's so much wild nonsense," he said. "Smart fellow like you, with all you know of history and the world." There was at least as much bitterness in his voice when he described me thus as there was affection, but I had grown accustomed to it in the years since my schooling and by then I barely noticed it.

"I don't think that at all," I said. "I think it's extremely interesting."

"Good," said my pa and I could see that he really was pleased in spite of his gruffness. "You believe he was telling the truth?"

"Oh, as he saw it, most certainly," I said. "But you must remind me… what was he like when you met him? Mr Malone?

How did he seem to you when you brought him that night to the station?"

So my father was able to tell the story of the arrest again and of the discovery of Malone's body the following morning. And this comforted him in a way and it comforted me too, truth be told, as the sound of his voice brought me back to my childhood when the world seemed a simpler place, when my parents were immutable and without flaw.

From that night on, the scrapbook became, in an odd fashion, our friend, a close companion of us both, discussion of which could be relied upon to fill any awkward silence or to dilute those instances when our mutual irritation threatened to boil over into something worse.

Its chief players were Crowe, the doomed and I presumed fraudulent "prophet"; Malone, the richest beggar in NYC; Greene, philanderer and murderer; the man who gave his name as Victor Frankenstein for all that the logs of the Walton expedition of 1799 (for I have seen these now for myself) claim unequivocally that the gentleman in question died on board, held fast amongst the ice.

At this early stage, I cannot say quite how seriously I took it or whether I treated it more as a kind of parlour game to help my father in the wake of his bereavement. What I do know for certain is that it worked on me slowly just as it had on my pa before me, with all its subtle horrors and unanswered questions. I was aware too that this was not to my father a document that spoke only of the past, for all that its leading characters were all deceased. Some part of him seemed certain that, whatever the truth of what had come to pass in Crispin Rye, it was not yet done with.

From time to time, in between (I suspected) his various and faintly undignified liaisons, he would arrive on my doorstep with an article from a newspaper which had caught his eye or some piece of gossip from an old colleague whispered at the end of a reunion supper. On the surface, these might seem strange or sad — some vandalism in a graveyard, say, or a figure glimpsed at dawn down by a culvert, moving with an odd, lurching, scuttling motion, scouring the shore with unfathomable purpose. I was aware, of course, that he saw some pattern, or at least an echo of the Malone case, in it all, though I had not the time to indulge his theories (or so, at least, I tell myself) because of my fledgling career (along with an equally fledgling and ultimately unsuccessful romance with a lovely young woman from Illinois).

All of which brings me back to the night before my father died. He called unexpectedly, shortly before nine. I was reading through a volume of letters pertaining to the wild hysteria in Salem, Massachusetts (and dreaming, just a little, perhaps, of that Illinois beauty) when I heard a hammering upon the door.

This was the November of 1870 and my father had been getting worse ever since the springtime at least. His visits to me had grown in intensity just as they had diminished in frequency. The sense that he was piecing together some larger picture which was in truth mostly illusory had grown more strong to me, and the connections at which he now grabbed seemed ever more desperate, contradictory and disordered than before. I dare say that I should have done more to help him but I did not know how.

On the evening in question, he bustled in, flourishing a copy of the *Herald* and drawing attention to a piece of reporting concerning the disappearance of several corpses at one of the city's busiest morgues. I asked him to sit down and take a drink so that we might discuss it all clear-sightedly but it was as though he did not hear me.

He was pacing and sighing, and thinking out loud, seemingly barely aware that I was there. He was badly unshaven. His hair was too long and his clothes looked dirty, even soiled. My mother would have been very sad, I thought, to have seen him so reduced.

At last, he stopped his pacing and he looked me in the eye. "So," he said, "we're agreed, are we, that Victor put his own brain into the body of Hubert Crowe? That, knowing his age and frailty, he made sure of his own survival that way?"

The implication of Malone's account had always been clear and we had said as much before.

"Well, poor Mr Malone evidently believed just that," I said carefully so as not to rile up my father any further.

"And that this... makeshift Creature somehow followed Malone here?"

"Yes," I said, adding: "though his diary is clearly not the work of a well man."

My pa just snorted at this. "He's started again," he said. "Victor. He's here and he's started again. Building. New creatures. New children."

His eyes were very wide. I worried for him.

"Pa," I said. "Let me get you a drink. Rest your feet. You're welcome to stay here for tonight if you'd care to. Take a bath."

My father looked at me then with cold contempt. "You think I'm mad?"

"Of course not. But you do look tired."

"Can't sleep," he said. "Can't sleep. Not when I know he's out there. That he's been out there all this long while. Underground. You see? That's where he's gone."

"Pa…" I said gently. "They're all dead. If there was ever any real truth in it they are surely now all dead and gone…"

He shook his head. "You're wrong," he said simply, "and you're a fool to boot." Then he turned and he left my apartment and those words were the last he ever spoke to me.

I called after him but he did not reply. I should have followed but I did not do so, stung, I suppose, by what he had said. That this decision is also a source of enduring regret to me should be obvious.

They found his body the following evening, down by the bay. He had drowned. There were no signs of violence on his body. They sent an old colleague of his to give me the news – a man called Keeney. He asked me if I had known any reason why my father would ever have got so close to the water's edge. I lied and said that there was none I could think of.

"An accident then," Keeney said uncertainly. "A tragic accident."

We looked at one another and each of us knew, more or less, what the other was thinking.

So we buried my father and my life went on. Four women whose names I didn't know attended the funeral. My own romance wilted and died. My career reached an impasse. My pa had no money or property to leave me but he did bequeath me that scrapbook.

In the twenty-four months which have gone by since his passing I have returned more often to it than I ought and I have found myself, at first in lopsided memory of my pa and then in genuine, quickening interest, conducting researches of my own.

Much of the story can be authenticated and I have found proof that many of those involved all lived and died at roughly the times that Malone had claimed.

Then I began to notice what my father had noticed before me — an almost invisible pattern of events right here in New York City: whispers of experiments below the streets; a tall man with a scarred face rumoured to be offering money for grave robbing and parts; disturbances in graveyards, in the sewers, by the bay, under bridges; a rash of murder victims, all unconnected save for disturbingly similar mutilations and removals.

In the time that these realisations have occurred to me I have also come to understand that I have no-one at all in my life to whom I might vouchsafe them. I dare not go to the police for they will surely think me mad. I might be incarcerated or worse. I have few friends and no close ones who might, if not believe my story, then at least give me a fair hearing.

No, I am in every way alone and isolated.

Or so, at least, I thought until yesterday night.

This, then, is why I have written this little piece of memoir and wrapped it around the scrapbook of Jesse Malone. This is why I have left it with a reputable attorney with instructions to publish in the event of my death or unexplained disappearance. This is why, as I write these last words, I do so with a bag packed beside me, with a stout pair of boots upon my feet and with a gun in my jacket pocket.

For tonight, I am to descend into the city. Underground is where he has made his lair. I have no doubt of that. Evil, festering evil, under the greatest city on God's earth.

But I will not make this descent alone. There are those who will go with me.

Last night, they came to my door, late, after midnight, under cover of darkness. Their knocking woke me from bad dreams. I had dozed in my armchair, that scrapbook on my knees. I stole to the door and opened it, knowing somehow that the visitors were of no ordinary sort and that my life was about to be forever changed.

And there they were, standing on my threshold – the great, tall, yellow-eyed Creature who had been made in Ingolstadt so long ago and, beside him, the boy, Adam, made in Crispin Rye in 1843. Their eyes glittered with uncanny knowledge.

"Dr Wyatt?" said the elder Creature, as courteous as an undertaker.

"Yes…" I said, thinking in that moment of terrible revelation only of my father. "That's me."

"Can we come inside?" he asked, his voice low and somehow thrilling. "For we have much to discuss and there is much we have to accomplish in this city."

And so I let them both in and we spoke and I saw the full truth of it at last.

This account is all done now. The facts are here for any who cares to see.

And by the time that you read this (whoever you may be), matters will finally be settled – one way or the other, for good or for ill.

Dr Frank Wyatt

NEW YORK,
OCTOBER 30TH, 1872

ACKNOWLEDGEMENTS

Thanks to my agent, Alexander Cochran; my editor, Daniel Carpenter; my patient wife, Heather, and our little Creatures, Alistair and Ben. Thanks also to D. J. Taylor, a regular source of support and inspiration.

ABOUT THE AUTHOR

J. S. Barnes is the author of five previous novels including *Dracula's Child* and *The City of Dr Moreau*. His journalism has appeared in the *Times Literary Supplement*, *The Critic* and the *Spectator*. He lives in Norfolk.

Also available from Titan Books

THE GHOSTS OF MERRY HALL

Heather Davey

In the present day, following the break-up of a controlling marriage, single mother Nell moves into the crumbling Victorian Merry Hall with her teenage daughter, Fern. She's determined to make a new life but the noises, moving objects, and strange smells in her new home make her increasingly unsettled.

In the 1840s, showman Abel Wenham seduces Dolly, a talented albino girl and makes her the star of his performing collection of 'freaks'. But after she becomes pregnant with his child, he discards her and imprisons her at Merry Hall, where her only solace is the company of fellow performers Ada the Bear Lady and the Jack the Posturer. They plan to escape with Dolly and her child and set up in business, but Wenham has other ideas.

When Fern admits she, too, is pregnant, it seems as though history may be about to repeat itself. But is Dolly, just one of the ghosts that haunt Merry Hall, reaching out across the centuries to protect her own child?

Told in alternating chapters across two timelines – one in the mid-19th century, one in the present day – this page-turning gothic chiller is ideal for those who love *The Whistling* by Rebecca Netley, *The Whispering Muse* by Laura Purcell and *The Wayward Girls* by Amanda Mason.

- TITANBOOKS.COM -

Also available from Titan Books

JEKYLL & HYDE: CONSULTING DETECTIVES

Tim Major

"A wonderful concept, beautifully executed."
Jeremy Dyson

When Muriel Carew attends a lavish society party, the last person she expects to bump into is her ex-fiancée Henry Jekyll, a man she's not seen for many years. When Jekyll turns out to be investigating a series of missing persons in London, Muriel is intrigued. But Jekyll is not working alone, and if Muriel wants to aid in the investigation, she must work with both Henry and his partner, the monstrous and uncouth Mr Hyde.

As their search takes a dark turn and a missing persons case becomes a murder investigation, Muriel finds herself deep in a mystery involving a nefarious group exploring their own hidden alter-egos within the beating heart of London's high society.

To solve the case and bring those responsible to justice, Muriel must find a way to place her trust in Mr Hyde, which might mean uncovering secrets about her own life she never dreamed of discovering.

- TITANBOOKS.COM -

Also available from Titan Books

DRACULA'S CHILD

J. S. Barnes

"A boldly inventive sequel to Dracula rips along with a sustained energy and verve, twisting and turning all the way."
Times Literary Supplement

It has been some years since Jonathan and Mina Harker survived their ordeal in Transylvania and, vanquishing Count Dracula, returned to England to try and live ordinary lives.

But shadows linger long in this world of blood feud and superstition – and, the older their son Quincey gets, the deeper the shadows that lengthen at the heart of the Harkers' marriage. Jonathan has turned back to drink; Mina finds herself isolated inside the confines of her own family; Quincey himself struggles to live up to a family of such high renown.

And when a gathering of old friends leads to unexpected tragedy, the very particular wounds in the heart of the Harkers' marriage are about to be exposed...

There is darkness both within the marriage and without – for new evil is arising on the Continent. A naturalist is bringing a new species of bat back to London; two English gentlemen, on their separate tours of the Continent, find a strange quixotic love for each other, and stumble into a calamity far worse than either has imagined; and the vestiges of something forgotten long ago is finally beginning to stir...

- TITANBOOKS.COM -

For more fantastic fiction, author events,
exclusive excerpts, competitions, limited editions and more

VISIT OUR WEBSITE
titanbooks.com

LIKE US ON FACEBOOK
facebook.com/titanbooks

FOLLOW US ON TWITTER AND INSTAGRAM
@TitanBooks

EMAIL US
readerfeedback@titanemail.com